SWEET MARMALADE, SOUR ORANGES:

Contemporary Portuguese Women's Fiction

SWEET MARMALADE, SOUR ORANGES:

Contemporary Portuguese Women's Fiction

Edited with Introduction and Notes by
Alice Clemente

Gávea-Brown
Providence, Rhode Island

Cover and Design
 Sharon Allen

Published by
 Gávea-Brown Publications
 Department of Portuguese and Brazilian Studies
 Brown University
 Providence, Rhode Island 02912

Distributed by
 Luso-Brazilian Books
 538 State Street
 Brooklyn, New York 11217

© 1994 by Alice Clemente. All rights reserved.

Library of Congress Catalog Card Number 92-73209

ISBN 0-943722-20-9

To the memory of

Alipio R. Clemente
Maria J. Clemente
Helena J. Ferreira

CONTENTS

Introduction 9

The Golden Boys *(excerpt)*
        Agustina Bessa-Luís 21

"Mother, Mother, Why Have You Forsaken Me?"
        Natália Correia 37

The Master *(excerpt)*
        Ana Hatherly 59

The Woman Who Wanted To Die
        Maria Ondina Braga 73

        Over the Other Faded One *(excerpt)*
        Maria Isabel Barreno 85

Houses In the Shadow *(excerpt)*
        Maria Velho da Costa 97

Emma *(excerpt)*
        Maria Teresa Horta 121

Sweet Marmalade, Sour Oranges *(excerpt)*
        Olga Gonçalves 143

The Day of the Marvels *(excerpt)*
        Lídia Jorge 153

My Story, Your Story *(excerpt)*
        Eduarda Dionísio 167

Shimmering Umbrellas *(excerpt)*
        Teolinda Gersão 181

The Devil's Mountain *(excerpt)*
        Hélia Correia 201

About the Translators 215

INTRODUCTION

The peaceful revolution of April 25, 1974 served, as nothing else could, to bring Portugal into the modern world, not only in a political sense but technologically, economically, socially, and culturally. With it, half a century of dictatorship was brought definitively to an end and the seeds of democracy were sown. The new democratic regime, in its turn, gave the death blow to a second political institution that had kept Portugal mired in the past: it extricated the country from a colonial involvement that had devastated human resources in the quest for material gain. The immediate sacrifice was great. A small and relatively poor country, Portugal was forced to relinquish its extensive colonial holdings at the same time that it absorbed the large number of "returnee" families that had in many cases made their fortunes in Africa for generations. These people suddenly found themselves back in the homeland without means. In time, the country recovered sufficiently from the economic turmoil that ensued to win acceptance into the European Economic Community, its success buoyed in some measure by the initiative of those same enterprising individuals who had earlier invested their energies in the colonial enterprise.

At the same time that Portugal was transforming itself from a fading imperial power into a partner in a modern European community, an internal transformation was also taking place. The immediate response to release from the oppression of dictatorship was anarchy. Unbridled exuberance was short-lived, however, as the newly-empowered populace set about creating the free society that they envisioned as the hope for the future. A new constitution embodying the philosophy of the United Nations' Declaration of Human Rights and setting forth those rights in detail was adopted in 1976 and revised in 1982. Mechanisms were set up to implement the document, and individual members of society set about internalizing its ideas in their everyday lives. A free press put the country in touch with the rest of the world—with progressive notions of social change, as well as with advanced technology. Within ten years of the demise of the dictatorship, many of these had become a part of society's fabric.

As a group, women reaped considerable benefit from the new and enlightened vision. They became active participants in the processes of economic, social, and political change and the subject of particular attention for the framers of the Constitution. The Revolution was a major breakthrough in the long, painful struggle for equality that had seen its beginnings in the early decades of the century. To grasp the full significance of women's gains, we must set them within this broad context.

It was early in the twentieth century that Portuguese women began—very slowly—to find a place in the public sphere. In 1891, the first woman doctor was licensed. In 1911, the first university chair awarded to a woman was given to German-born Carolina Michaelis de Vasconcelos, wife of the noted Portuguese musicologist and art historian Joaquim de Vasconcelos. In 1913 the first woman lawyer received her degree. Under the influence of international women's movements, middle-class women began to organize. In 1909, they formed the Republican League of Portuguese Women, with Dr. Adelaide Cabete and the writer Ana de Castro Osório at its helm pleading the case for women's education. In 1914, the National Council of Portuguese Women, a branch of the International Women's Council, was founded by Adelaide Cabete, and in 1924, a congress on feminism and education was convoked. The period was ripe for social change: a liberal Republic had been established in 1910 following the assassination of the last monarch. The President of the Republic attended the women's conference, and its proceedings were covered daily in the press. These middle-class women led and won the fight for reform in family law, for improved conditions in the workplace, and for maternity care and equitable wages. In 1910, a divorce law for which women reformers had lobbied was passed, granting both husband and wife equal treatment under the law with respect to grounds and custody rights. Women were no longer required by law to obey their husbands. By 1920, girls were admitted to previously all-male secondary schools, and by 1926, women were allowed to

INTRODUCTION

teach there. Women were not yet able to vote, however. They did not receive that right until 1931. Typically, the franchise was restricted to women who had completed secondary education, though the requirement for men was only minimal literacy. Suffrage was a limited achievement for another reason: by 1926, the new regime that brought with it the dictatorship of António Oliveira de Salazar had already become a reality. The Estado Novo (New State), as it was called, virtually eradicated the other gains women had made. Its Constitution granted equality to all citizens "except with respect to women, the differences resulting from their nature and from the interests of the family" (Art. 5). A concordat between Portugal and the Vatican in 1950 abolished divorce. The National Council of Portuguese Women was also abolished and the family-oriented ideology of the dictator was imposed on the country.

In time, the late 1960s, the status of women began to rise once again. The push for social reform being what it was in the western world during that decade, it would have been difficult for even an isolationist dictatorship like that of Portugal to resist its influence. In 1967, a new Civil Code was promulgated. Women no longer needed their husbands' permission to work in the professions or in government offices; they were guaranteed equal pay for equal work. The Constitution, however, still stated that all citizens except women were equal under the law, the distinction being determined by a perceived difference in women's nature. It also stated that the husband was the head of the family and, as such, was empowered to decide and direct all matters concerning marital life. With the disappearance of Salazar from the political scene in 1968 and his replacement by the more moderate Marcelo Caetano came increased loosening of restrictions. Access to education for women had gradually improved and continued to do so, as did the awareness of women's special needs. In 1973, the Commission for Social Policy Concerning Women was formed. By coincidence, it was in that year that the famous "Three Marias" episode drew attention, nationally and internationally, to the plight of women in Portugal. In 1972, Maria Teresa Horta, Maria Isabel Barreno, and Maria Velho da Costa had published the product of their experiment in collective writing, *Novas Cartas Portuguesas* (*New Portuguese Letters*). While the book dealt with such diverse issues as the definition of self and other, the political and social situation of Portugal at that time, and the writing process itself, the explicit sexuality in its treatment of male-female relations, along with its obvious challenge to traditional values, brought upon its authors the wrath of the regime which, like its counterpart in Franco's Spain, was vehemently opposed to the erotic in art and literature. The book was confiscated by the police and a morals charge filed against the Three Marias. The international press took up the cause and in 1974 the women were exonerated. All things considered, it is no surprise that when the Revolution broke out on April 25, 1974, the status of women was on people's minds as one of the problems in need of correction. Efforts to address inequities began almost immediately. Some were spontaneous, as women took their place beside men in a variety of settings ranging from neighborhood organizations to the highest political offices. Women were elected to Parliament as well as to local office; these women addressed women's issues in the normal exercise of their duties. Others addressed them more exclusively through the Movimento da Libertação das Mulheres (Women's Liberation Movement). Still others worked through the Commission on the Status of Women, which was established by law in 1977, though it had begun to function earlier. One of its presidents was Maria Lurdes Pintassilgo, who became Prime Minister of Portugal in 1979. The Commission on the Status of Women lobbied successfully for improvements in education, health, maternity care, and family planning. In 1984, Zita Seabra, a powerful member of the Communist Party's Central Committee, led a successful fight for legalized abortion under specified conditions. Most importantly, the new constitution which came into force in 1976 was clear on women's rights. Article 13 stated: "No-one shall be privileged, favored, prejudiced, deprived of any right or exempt from any duty because of his ancestry, sex, race, language, territory of origin, religion, political or ideological convictions, education, economic situation or social condition." Article 36 stated that husbands and wives shall have equal rights and responsibilities with regard not only to civil and political matters but also to the care and education of their children. Article 48: "All citizens shall have the right to take part in the country's political life and in the running

INTRODUCTION

of its political affairs, either directly or through freely-elected representatives." The Constitution went on to specify the right to work, to an education, to maternity leave, and to child care, and mandated the establishment of structures needed to implement these new laws. Women thus achieved legal equality in a country that also ratified efforts on behalf of women in the United Nations and in the European Parliament. By 1985, women were sufficiently well-established in the power structure to enable Maria Lurdes Pintassilgo to run for the presidency of the country. She was unsuccessful in her bid but during that same year the then-President of the Republic decorated seven Portuguese women "who by 'promoting, improving and enhancing the status of women, have improved and dignified the status of all human beings'" (Commission on the Status of Women, *Portugal: Status of Women,* 1988). While the abuse of women was not eradicated completely with these reforms, efforts continued to be made to bring practice into line with policy.

The history of women's writing in Portugal runs parallel to the history of their success in the civil rights arena. In the early 1900s, the women's movement spoke officially through its own journals, *A Madrugada* (*Dawn*) and *Alma Feminina* (*Woman's Soul*). With two major exceptions, women's writing was in fact directly related to the women's movement. Dr. Adelaide Cabete and the journalist Maria Lamas, for example, published monographs on women's rights. The exceptions were Ana de Castro Osório (1872-1935) and Florbela Espanca (1894-1930), who were to forge a reputation far beyond the boundaries of the women's movement. Ana de Castro Osório was a prolific writer: essayist, short story writer, dramatist, and novelist. Her books for children were of major importance; one was adopted as a textbook in both Portugal and Brazil. The outstanding figure in that part of the century, however, was Florbela Espanca, unquestionably one of the greatest Portuguese poets of all time. Her tortured, erotic sonnets achieved immediate success and remain popular to this day, her works having been carefully re-edited in the 1980s.

With the advent of the Estado Novo, women's writing lost momentum both in quantity and in feminist orientation. Isolated voices continued to be heard; Irene Lisboa (1892-1958) was one of them. Lisboa pursued dual careers in education and in literature. She authored several books on pedagogical subjects as well as the literary works for which she is remembered. Often identified as a precursor of the Neo-Realist movement, Lisboa left behind a moving testimony to women's solitude *(Solidão, II,* 1966) that only in the 1980s received the attention it deserves. Women writers remained on the fringe of the literary world through the 1940s, but the 1950s opened a new era. In poetry, the important voice was that of Sophia de Melo Breyner Andresen (b. 1919), daughter of an aristocratic northern family, who studied Classics at the University of Lisbon and went on to write poetry influenced by her classical training. From early poetry that sang the beauty of physical reality, she moved towards an *oeuvre* that was moral and political in its orientation, championing those who struggled on behalf of human needs. More immediately and significantly political was Natália Correia (b. 1923), who was to cultivate not only poetry but also the short story, the novel, theater, literary scholarship, political writing, and indeed politics itself. From the beginning, she rebelled against oppression and asserted her individuality. She clashed openly with the regime and found her writing censored for its audacity. Some of her work was withdrawn from circulation and she was prosecuted for other pieces, most notably an anthology of erotic (male) poetry. Other significant names of this period were the novelist Fernanda Botelho (b. 1926) and the short-story writer Maria Judite de Carvalho (b. 1921), but most important of all in a purely literary sense was Agustina Bessa-Luís (b. 1922), who exploded on the literary scene in 1953 with her prize-winning novel *A Sibila* (*The Sibyl*). She became at once the center of polemical attention as she broke with the dominant literary currents of the day to set her own mark on the history of Portuguese fiction. These women, highly individualistic and highly independent, were pioneers and served as eventual role models for generations to come. Sophia de Melo Breyner Andresen and Natália Correia both became members of Parliament following the Revolution, and the latter continues to be a prominent figure in the world of politics. It was this Fifties generation that paved the way for the Three Marias and for the feminist writing of the early to mid-1970s. The *Novas Cartas Portuguesas* episode, vigorously supported by Natália Correia, was not an

INTRODUCTION

isolated incident but a beginning. Its legal ramifications were still in the process of resolution when the Revolution broke out, bringing with it yet another era in the history of women's writing: a profusion of new fiction by these now-familiar names as well as by a host of new talent.

The period following the *25 de Abril,* as the Revolution is commonly called, was an important one for feminism. The Three Marias were particularly active in the Movimento da Libertação das Mulheres; Maria Teresa Horta and Maria Isabel Barreno were its co-founders. They also continued to write feminist fiction accepted without reservation or restriction in the post-revolutionary era. These women in turn paved the way for yet another generation of writers free now to write as they would. Interestingly, this generation felt no compulsion to follow the political path of their feminist predecessors. The writing that resulted from their newly-acquired freedom was neither particularly erotic nor particularly militant. The younger writers, those who began to publish in the 1980s, have gone so far as to deny the very concept of women's writing. Teolinda Gersão and Hélia Correia are among the latter. For Lídia Jorge, the most admired of the younger writers, the perfect artist is the one who can overcome gender limits and capture the essence of another's experience, whether that other be male or female. "Aesthetic quality is supra-sexual," she has asserted. "The human word, when it attains a certain degree of strength, the power to produce dreams, has nothing to do with whether it is proffered by men or by women" ("A Surpresa no Feminimo," *Expresso,* February 5, 1983). African-born Wanda Ramos, on the other hand, has tempered her position, finding that while in its formal aspects women's writing cannot be set in opposition to men's writing, thematically there is a complementarity. For her, women's writing reflects women's place in the world as well as a characteristic way of approaching life's problems. While the writers of all three of the generations writing after the Revolution tended to privilege women protagonists and women's experience, most would agree with Lídia Jorge that in the 1980s —precisely because of the militancy of Natália Correia and the Three Marias—it is no longer necessary for women to write gender-dominated fictions as earlier feminists did. Women are free to be writers, purely and simply, as are their male counterparts. The reading public would seem to agree. The new fiction by women has found strong critical and commercial support; its authors have earned universal respect, in some cases to a level of veneration virtually unknown in the past. Portuguese women's fiction of the post-revolutionary years, like that of the men, has been marked by developments in the novel beyond the country's borders. Its authors have obviously read the *nouveau roman* and the literature of the Latin American Boom, as well as the early Agustina Bessa-Luís. They have to a woman adopted narrative techniques that place them closer to these than to the Realism and Neo-Realism that preceded them. Narrative discontinuity, for example, is prevalent in their work, as is a metafictional challenging of traditional models. While these techniques have served them well in their exposé of the inner realities of women's lives, they have been equally appropriate for their treatment of the multifaceted political and social reality that surrounds them and that so obviously captured their imagination in the early years of the post-revolutionary period. Within these common lines, the differences have been great, ranging from the cerebral mythical constructs of an Agustina Bessa-Luís to the controlled fantasies of Lídia Jorge and Hélia Correia, the testimonial fictions of Olga Gonçalves, and the word-play and formal experiments of Maria Velho da Costa.

In putting together this anthology of contemporary Portuguese women's fiction, I have chosen to concentrate on the post-revolutionary period, in part because some of the earlier writing is already available in English. See, for example, the *Longman Anthology of World Literature by Women* (ed. Marian Arkin and Barbara Shollar, 1988). It seemed, furthermore, that it would be illuminating to see the kinds of writing that are produced when after a period of severe oppression women are suddenly free to speak in a climate that is at once expansive and receptive. Focusing on a single timeframe also gives cohesiveness to an otherwise amorphous collection of texts. The selection of the dozen authors represented here is not meant to be in any sense inclusive but responds rather to spatial constraints. There are other writers who could well have been included; Maria Gabriela Llansol, Maria Judite de Carvalho, Fernanda Botelho, and Clara Pinto Correia are among the most ob-

INTRODUCTION

vious omissions. One writer has been included who perhaps should not have been, Ana Hatherly, since her fiction does not technically belong to this period. Her only novel was selected because although it was published in the 1960s, it received little critical attention until the post-revolutionary era. It was a revolutionary work in its day. Hatherly, who was at the center of the experimental poetry movement, decided to experiment with fiction as well, utilizing some of the same poetic techniques in her novel. Consequently, she conceived a work that is formally and thematically more consonant with Portuguese fiction of the 1970s than with that of the 1960s. Finally, while acknowledging that it might have been preferable to translate works in their entirety—short stories, novellas—I concluded that this was neither possible nor advisable in all cases, since not all of the writers have published short stories, nor indeed is short fiction their forte. It is the novel that is the dominant fictional form of the post-revolutionary period. Hopefully, this anthology will be a first step in creating a market for those complete translations in the near future.

In closing, I would like to thank the authors and their publishers for graciously allowing me to include their works; the Commission on the Status of Women, which, with its excellent library and publications, provided much of the information brought together in this essay; the translators for generously and effectively executing their assignments; and Onésimo T. Almeida and his staff at Gávea/Brown for seeing the work through to publication.

A.R.C.

THE GOLDEN BOYS

(excerpt)

by

Agustina Bessa-Luís

AGUSTINA BESSA-LUÍS

Agustina Bessa-Luís was born into a well-established family in the northern rural region of Amarante in 1922. Basically autodidactic, perhaps because of the conservative ambiance in which she was raised, she is nevertheless the most purely intellectual of all contemporary Portuguese novelists, male and female. A person of wide-ranging curiosity and acute critical power, she is exceptionally well-read in a seemingly infinite variety of subjects.

Agustina Bessa-Luís began publishing in 1948 and five years later made literary history. Her novel A Sibila *(The Sibyl, 1953) signalled a radical break with the neo-realism that dominated the literary scene at that time. The critical controversy that ensued catapulted her into an international limelight. By 1959, she was sufficiently well known to be invited as the representative of Portugal to the Lourmarin writers' conference sponsored by the Faculty of Letters of Aix-en-Provence. This was the first of many significant excursions outside of the country both as tourist and as professional writer. A particularly significant voyage in the latter capacity took her to Israel in 1973 to participate in the World Conference of Women Writers and Journalists. In 1980, she was initiated by the then-president of Portugal, Ramalho Eanes, as a Grand Officer of the Military Order of Sant'Iago da Espada. Beginning with* A Sibila *her novels have won most of the major prizes awarded to fiction in her country.*

A prolific writer, Agustina Bessa-Luís has published some thirty novels, a half-dozen biographies, plays, essays, and stories. As emanations of a powerful intellect that often exhibits the sibylline qualities common to some of her protagonists, her writings are complex, dense works that break with traditional concepts of time, space, and authorial distance. They delve into the subliminal forces of human relations and human essences in a manner that Alvaro Manuel Machado, the author of two books on her work, has compared to that of Marguerite Yourcenar and even to Marcel Proust. The subject of Bessa-Luís's fictional inquiry was initially the complex closed matriar-

chal society of the Douro region in which she was raised, but increasingly she has broadened her vision geographically and temporally. Many of her later works, fictional and biographical, have dealt with historical figures from the Middle Ages and the seventeenth and eighteenth centuries as well as modern times but always the intention is the same: to reach a profound understanding of the passions, internal and external, by which these figures are driven. The boundaries between fiction and biography in her work are tenuous, blurred in both cases by omnipresent analytical authorial intrusions. Agustina Bessa-Luís has had a profound influence on the women writers of the two generations that have followed her. They look to her as a role model both as a writer and as a person who is intensely independent and audacious.

The selection translated here was taken from the novel Os Meninos de Ouro *(The Golden Boys, 1983), based on the life of Francisco Sá-Carneiro, the charismatic leader of the Social Democrats, who met an untimely death in a plane crash in 1980. While the novel ostensibly deals with the male protagonist, here, as often in Bessa-Luís's novels, it is the woman at the center of the man's life, his wife Rosamaria, who is the true center of the novel.*

Works by Agustina Bessa-Luís

Fiction

Mundo Fechado, *1948*
Os Super-Homens, *1950*
Contos Impopulares, *1951-53*
A Sibila, *1954*
Os Incuráveis, *1956*
A Muralha, *1957*
O Susto, *1958*
Ternos Guerreiros, *1960*
O Manto, *1961*
O Sermão do Fogo, *1962*
A Brusca, *1971*
As Pessoas Felizes, *1975*

AGUSTINA BESSA-LUÍS

Crónica do Cruzado Osb., *1976*
As Fúrias, *1977*
Fanny Owen, *1979*
O Mosteiro, *1980*
Os Meninos de Ouro, *1983*
Adivinhas de Pedro e Inês, *1983*
Um Bicho da Terra, *1984*
A Monja de Lisboa, *1985*
A Corte do Norte, *1987*
Prazer e Glória, *1988*
Eugénia e Silvina, *1989*
Vale Abraão, *1991*

As Relações Humanas:
I - Os Quatro Rios, *1964*
II - A Dança das Espadas, *1965*
III - Canção Diante de uma Porta Fechada, *1966*

A Bíblia dos Pobres:
I - Homens e Mulheres, *1967*
II - As Categorias, *1970*

Theater

O Inseparável, *1958*
A Bela Portuguesa, *1986*

Essays and Biography

Embaixada a Calígula, *1961*
Santo António, *1973*
Florbela Espanca, *1979*
Conversações com Dimitri e Outras Fantasias, *1979*
Sebastião José, *1981*
Longos Dias Têm Cem Anos, *1982*
Apocalipse de Albrecht Durer, *1986*

THE GOLDEN BOYS

It would please me very much to draw up an inventory, from the beginning to the end of this novel, of the genial and productive life of Ana de Cales, who was full of perseverance and of the mystique of a winner. Not without good reason did I inquire into the character of this Douro Amazon and her talent for business, which is the equivalent of the urban art of war that progressively developed until it became part of the terrorism waged from offices so dear to men who wield international power. Perhaps a more delicate subject than the one I propose to deal with would be that of the contemporary barons of politics, their accidents and misfortunes. But this would have made it impossible for me to portray the crude individual plus woman, judge of remote experience, who is going to be the main heroine of this book without having related her to Ana de Cales, her great-great-great-grandmother, provided the record is properly

---

From *Os Meninos de Ouro* (*The Golden Boys*), by Agustina Bessa-Luís (Lisbon: Guimarães, 1955).

checked. In 1955, the year when Maria Rosamaria Alba Pereira married a young doctor of law, Ana de Cales's picture (a photograph, not a portrait by Roquemont, as one would expect) displayed the remarkable resemblance to the bride. It was the same lean physique and eyes with a suspect brightness; it was the bony face, not without the elegance of the jawbone where the nerves moved as though by means of a precise and vibrant mechanism. Maria Rosamaria was the granddaughter of Hipólita Alba Pereira and, on a November afternoon, she joined her little dark and skinny hand to the most promising of husbands: José Moreira Matildes, of the Matildes of Santa Catarina, owners of an old Oporto estate that stretched from near Fradelos to Santo Ildefonso. He was an auspicious young man who had had an academic career in Coimbra without failing any courses and who, without being conspicuous, exhibited a potential very rare among Portuguese: power for him was not a consequence of his belonging to the dominant class but a destiny to be fulfilled, with all its misfortunes and disappointments, its greatnesses and displeasures. He was, in short, one of the few individuals who looked favorably upon the tragedy the country has produced since Alcacer-Kibir or since Dom Pedro V.

José Matildes, who was of medium height, something he valued so much that he stood very straight and walked with his shoulders pulled back, had received a traditional education, even too intransigent during a period when, due to the phenomenon of perfusion that the war had brought about in a country that had not participated in it, people took lightly even matters regarding God and death. The war, especially after the disclosure and spread of the concentration camps, when everything assumed an aura of unbearable reality that one approached as cultural study and not as convenient pain, had created in Portugal the defensive spirit which is benevolence without virtue and activism without a cause. José Matildes was a young man who differed from those who are ambitious due to depression and who use success as a cure for the slights inflicted on others by their families. A descendant of a keen-witted family from the border with Spain, for whom pride was a kind of hereditary disease whose symptoms might be either a sense of occupational pride or an extravagant and wounded reverence for their own indiscretions, Matildes became acquainted, through marriage, with the first danger that confronts men of passion: he made a blind example of marital fidelity, and let his wife, Rosamaria, embody the consciousness of the optimum limits of an exceptional citizen. To the common citizen belonged adultery, versatility of the spirit and of the flesh, and freedom—libidinous, economic, and emotional. For José Moreira Matildes, marriage was like an ordination. Besides fidelity, nothing existed for him save a liking for books and the rearing of his children. At the peak of his prosperity, he dedicated himself to collecting thirteenth- and sixteenth-century religious statues and silver objects related to the wine-growing industry—shears and *tomboladeiras*. They first resided in an old house that belonged to Grandmother Hipólita in the section by the river where the English middle class lived. The area was damp and frequented by people of dubious reputation, because the demolitions and the city's expropriation of the old estates had left the neighborhood without police protection. The area being deserted, the dangers did not justify the risks to the police. Even before the April Twenty-Fifth Revolution, assaults and sex offenses had taken place in this magnificent scenic area with many streets called "Lovers' Lane." After the Revolution of carnations, a licentiousness that led to exhibitionism spread to the grounds of Massarelos, and the drug traffic actually took over those parks still recognizable in the areas spared by urban depredations. Great ornamental trees rose against the narrow river inlet. There was still not much traffic on the bridge and Senhor Gustavo, who was a railroad retiree and with a mien like a Dickens criminal, that is to say, of a Jewish Fagin without a gang, would enjoy himself by counting the cars going over the upper level; he would place bets against himself, spending his time on this playful and private fantasy. At other times, he would invent or recognize sexual perverts ogling solitary couples. He would shout to expose them, though what he wanted was to grab the attention of the lovers, who always got carried away in their raptures and who seemed not to care about the oglers and the weary and scandal-deprived busybodies who came out to hang clothes on the lines. Heavy-clothed children singing the latest record hits would stare as though they were watching cock fights. The love pairs were the "double-backed creature" who had amused Rabelais and now amused them as well.

"Get out of there, shameless creatures!" Gustavo screamed. His fury left them indifferent.

"Leave us alone," replied a little blond and emaciated boy. He was as mean as the plague and would smear people's doors with excrement. But this fellow Rosamaria protected; she liked his uncompromising meanness, even though he also got on her nerves at times. She would see him carrying a bucket of scraps on those red afternoons of summer, and she felt sorry for him. But the boy, who was not more than six, would stop and stare at her.

"What is this piece of shit doing here?" he would say loudly in order to be heard by some shyer and less street-wise companion. At other times, when Rosamaria was wearing her beautiful fox coat, which she would put on to come out and get the mail, he would blurt out: "You look like a beehive!"—which surely bothered the recently married young woman. But she realized she was dealing with a brave boy; for sure, he would end up badly, misunderstood by a society unaccustomed to such juicy things as the spirit of that little fellow.

"I have never managed to have him tell me his name. He looks as though his name might be John," said Rosamaria. She was speaking to herself; even when her husband was present, he did not acknowledge her festive talkativeness mixed with laughter and witticisms. She was not a very well-read woman, and life for her consisted of a string of ridiculous things to which she sometimes felt the need to lend some formality. Hence she was a great observer of rituals and conventions, and lived solemnly in the midst of a conservative middle class full of facile lyricism. She did not fail to laugh about everything unabashedly; and even her love for her children, which she defined as a miracle, something dictated by her special charisma, that of a prudent and sovereign mother, was to some degree her way of excusing herself for a kind of gloomy lucidity with which she sometimes observed them. Notwithstanding the many years that separated them, Rosamaria was the incarnation of Ana de Cales in all her formidable personality, something between the barbarian and the omniscient. No one could claim to know her well, so disarming, spiteful, perturbing, and bewitching was she in the crudest sense of the word. She did not love without hurting, and did not favor anyone without regretting it. With her, José

THE GOLDEN BOYS

Matildes found an unaltered, chaste, balanced, and exemplary happiness. Rosamaria's ignorance guaranteed him the kind of servitude that intellectuals appreciate in their intimate relations. There isn't a man of letters who sees in letters anything except a tool and not a state of grace. And if he is surrounded by mediocre people, even stupid people, his spirit does not suffer; he even delights in this and enjoys it, because learned men are like rich men who, in a world of generalized opulence, neither find pleasure in nor measure for their profits. Still, Rosamaria possessed a degree of understanding much superior to that measured by any formal knowledge. She was a woman capable of great things, provided their nature was not to impart information; which is to say that her pride was her absolute reason for existing. Language would necessarily be viewed by her as a vehicle for the propagation of commonness and, therefore, all learning was a form of subservience, something vile.

It was inevitable that one day the couple would arrive at a discovery: that their love was a farce, and that the only thing left to them was a muffled and prickly conscience that would ruin them, "if God should grant them a long and healthy life," in Rosamaria's spirited and crazy way of being facetious. Meanwhile they lived cautiously, avoiding relations with strangers and forbidding themselves any situations involving surprises. During fifteen years of marriage they kept to themselves, educating their children, two boys and a girl, and rarely visiting relatives. Once, when Uncle Mateus, having divorced Aura, spent time at their home, José came down with an illness that left the doctors bewildered and which lasted until the memory of its first symptoms vanished and it was no longer possible to draw up a coherent medical report. José was overcome by sharp abdominal pains, and tests revealed a rare case of rotting of the intestine. He had an operation and seemed to recover. However, months later, nine to be exact, he had a relapse and underwent another operation. Mateus got a position in a bank in Paris, which was considered most fortunate by those who were acquainted with his eccentricities, and José gradually recovered. It was not a spectacular recovery, but by March 1967 he was leading a normal life and attending to his high-finance clients, who forced him to undertake successive trips abroad. He was a legal consultant for various companies, some multinational, and earned a lot of money. Aside from a certain inclination for collecting, not devoid of the pleasure of speculation, he was not a spendthrift, and Rosamaria herself was actually a tightwad. A dress would last her five years, and she would buy shoes in flea markets, where she got involved in great bargaining rounds with the gypsies and their massive spouses, who ended up by allowing her to try on big golden pendants and enormous aprons. Rosamaria delighted in this promiscuity and would say that "the stench alone was enough to generate fleas." She liked those who lived outside the mainstream, cheats, those accustomed to intrigues and swindles; she liked above all to unravel their ploy, to watch the latter turn into a more or less well-executed scheme. The bill rapidly exchanged for another of lesser value; the slippery hand delicately picking a wallet; the disturbance meant to distract attention and allow for a swift move, like plucking a pair of earrings off a child or cutting a necklace off a maid.

"Dear lady, check this incorrect change." She would open her hand without looking suspicious, happy to confront the cunning of the saleswomen, their tricks, their art of loading the scales and of pressing down on one of the pans with their thumb to make it weigh more.

At times, Rosamaria would invent perfect mornings: she herself would steal a little for the sake of winning a round, of gambling for high stakes, of outdoing the professionals. She would tell José, who thought she was ignoble.

"You are a gambler, for sure, and you don't accept blame or criticism. That is what's unforgivable," he said. Rosamaria laughed at him.

"I'm not going to miss my chance. Everybody does it."

"No, not everybody."

"Even God. Even you." She looked at him as if to discover the effect of her words, which she knew would go against his scruples, but he did not react. Perhaps he drew some satisfaction from his wife's crazy logic, and perhaps she loosened his obsessive severity that seemed useless and disorganized. "I love you," she said suddenly. She sat on the floor between his knees and he felt overcome by his emotions, like a puff of cold air that set his hair on end. He desired to kiss her but did not, because that would amount to giving in to her own invitation. He was of the opinion that love had to be cultivated in such a way so as not to consume and lead a man from the path of intelligence. He said disapprovingly:

"Why did you stop wearing mourning clothes?"

She looked surprised, then she remembered Carmina's death, which had happened almost a year before. She was her great-aunt, Hipólita's sister, and no one would expect her to wear black for very long. After all, since the family was so big, it would keep her in perpetual mourning because deaths occurred frequently. Rosamaria would say that it was good to have clothes other than black, for any eventuality.

"And the uncles and aunts have not started dying yet. You will see when we get together on Sundays how we resemble a House of Bernarda Alba."

Mateus was the one who compared her to the daughters of Bernarda Alba, and José felt uncomfortable remembering that. Mateus had opposed his marriage; a brother of Rosamaria's own mother, he had her in mind for his and Aura's only son. Since that did not happen, he started having marital problems and separated from his wife when he was still a good-looking man with pretensions of being elegant. He was, in fact, one of the last dandies in the city; he was cynical and ill-tempered, and had fits of great generosity. He cultivated contradictions and harbored no guilt feelings about anything.

"Good men contribute to the unreality of institutions. They are like camels who are never thirsty."

"What do you mean by that?" asked Hipólita, invariably ill-humored and stiff-necked, though pretending to be more austere than she wanted to be.

"Nothing. Not even in dreams do camels mean anything. There are no camels in the theory of interpretation of dreams."

"Why are you speaking about camels, then?"

"I am a nomad, that's why camels mean much to me."

"Silly!" said Hipólita. This was the kind of dialogue that

mother and son sustained regularly. After the deaths of António and Inácio, whom she missed excessively, even to the point of compromising her relationships to those who were still living, she would fall into a kind of guilt feeling about Mateus; she would ransack her memory in search of minor inattentions and even cruelties toward that son whose love she now found indispensable. She forgave him everything, even the famous separation from Aura, her godchild, whom Hipólita had "shocked," that's the word, by offering her consecutively to each of her sons, as if she were a gold watch or a chain with a medallion. For sure, not even Mateus knew why he had rejected his wife. Caustic as he was, he always treated her well, distinguishing her with the affection due a sister-in-law and not with the love deserved by a wife. He gave her a lot of attention, not even fearing to appear overly sentimental in public, and he immensely appreciated the inheritance she she had brought him. With no children, married first to António and then to Inácio, she had received a colossal patrimony from both, which made her one of the richest women in the country. Aura had maintained her beauty as another patrimony, and her repeated marriages did not seem ridiculous. Her extremely humble albeit not dishonorable beginnings remained buried in a past to which only Hipólita kept the key. There were those who claimed that Aura was her daughter, born within wedlock but, in fact, sired by her handsome foreman, who had died without receiving much care in an estate adjacent to the Cales's which, extravagantly, was the property of the oldest member of any family living there. José Matildes, pettifogger that he was, tried to contest that clause stemming from Ana de Cales's will, but came up against a kind of mystic respect for the proprietress that was shared by the whole family. She had had a patriarchal vision of protection toward her descendants, which extended beyond her love for her offspring. All her grandchildren came under the umbrella of the enormous emporium of her fortune, which she had the genius to protect within a cleverly organized society of shareholders. For many years that system of tutelage had saved from ruin the most adventuresome or destitute of her progeny. This included those who married (more or less ruined title-holders) below their class, and those who got involved in speculative ventures and lawsuits; or the spendthrifts and the

THE GOLDEN BOYS

bons vivants who lived abroad in turreted *manoirs* with servants looking like wax figures—all were saved from indigence thanks to the articles of the Society which encompassed numerous estates and wine warehouses. Other names and fortunes came her way and tried to impose themselves; but Ana de Cales always remained the great symbol of the Douro orthodoxy, prudent, addicted to the ways of absolutism, according to which a mistake is justified as a dynamic objective. Above all, she had attained a local immortality, the type that affects the imagination of the common man and makes him feel that a neighbor's success is a pledge of destiny. This does not free him from a sense of inferiority but allows him to live with it as with a good neighbor.

When he married Rosamaria, José Matildes did not, really, strike an enviable financial deal. She was the daughter of Irene Alba Pereira, who had married a military man, Brigadier Nunes, a person obsessed with questions of honor and who felt contempt for money. He had built his career overseas and had become governor of Mozambique. The colonial war had made a neurasthenic of him, a bitter man empty of ideas. He had witnessed all kinds of corruption, he was well-acquainted with the contrabandists, who sometimes included even some high members of the clergy. He drank dry martinis with them at sunset, listened to their sensible and precautious pronouncements. Only his cook, by the name of Boné Julião, seemed to him a worthy person.

"Tell me, Boné: would you be capable of killing me?" The black man opened his eyes as big as headlights, and answered,

"Boss, forgive the black man but, if the black man has to kill the boss, he'll do it. I can't make exceptions, it doesn't look fair."

Irene, who appeared to be scorched by the African sun and who was skinny and dark as a scorpion, was filled with panic at this stage.

"I'm not going to stay here with you, I am sorry. This place is for mercenaries or lunatics."

She left by boat with her youngest children, her fine Chinese porcelain dinner and breakfast sets, in addition to her Shantung silks and some pearls. The brigadier remained; he drank his whiskey regularly and began to spend time at the home of a merry and sentimental Englishwoman.

"These shitty people from the mainland!" the brigadier would say when he needed to get it off his chest. The Englishwoman laughed while strolling naked in the living room decorated with paper lanterns. She was a really attractive woman, because she was neither too dramatic nor too venal; except for the question of Edward VIII's abdication, nothing seemed to bother her.

Until she married, Rosamaria spent all her time at Grandmother Hipólita's. She had been educated in mediocre schools, always commuting and staying at the Ramada Alta house, which the Alba Pereiras used in their frequent trips as a place to stop and change. Aura spent the entire winter there and, while she was married to António, most of the year. She and Inácio did not use this house much, for he was more restless and fond of the capital, where he frequented revue shows not lacking in interest because of popular pretty actresses who never played anything except bit parts but who ended up marrying rich and dull-witted men. Big, with verandas decorated with tiles looking like apron stripes, the Ramada Alta house was, at that time, still comfortable, despite the steep stairs in the style of Amsterdam dwellings. The kitchen was in the cellar, and the kitchen dumbwaiter was so big that a four-year-old could fit in it. Rosamaria had fun acting as a delicacy, and was hoisted by the errand boy Aristides, a sly and pretty child who later became the lover of a well-to-do old man who adopted him. Aristides adored Rosamaria, and she thought he was the best of friends; amusing as a goblin, he was capable of suffering the strangest humiliations in order for her to keep him as her confidant and messenger. During puberty, when she fell in love with all the boys of the neighborhood, even with Inácio and Mateus, who were notorious heartbreakers, Aristides would bring her, together with breakfast, the brief, dry, and urgent letters from her little lovers. She would press them to her breast, exaggerating her rapture, looking askance at Aristides who, pale with jealousy, pretended to side with her.

THE GOLDEN BOYS

"Aren't they silly? They say they love me. . . ." She jumped out of bed, put on a faded bathrobe, for Grandmother Hipólita did not allow her either luxuries or wastefulness. She had never wanted for that granddaughter either Swiss boarding schools or German governesses, as her cousins had had. They were the daughters of Isabel, who was called "the Dessert" because she was as sweet and decorated as a dessert. Aristides was used to those holiday mornings when Rosamaria would call him to wash her hair. He had light hands and never tired of rubbing raw eggs and beer on her hair to bring out its golden reflections. But the time when he was truly indispensable was at evening gatherings, when Grandmother Hipólita was already asleep buried in a large old chair with the pages of the newspaper lying about her, like petals scattered by the wind. Rosamaria, who had serious whims and was as lazy as a Moor, would ask him to scratch her back, cut her toenails, remove dark spots from her nose, even from inside her ears where the soap had created a greasy crust and where a layer of dandruff had accumulated like a thin flake of unmelted snow. Aristides obliged her; and never, as a married woman content with her pleasures, did she experience that abbatial satisfaction, that abandoning of her body to its caretaker who was, more than a lover, a tiny jockey of her caprices and of appetites in which the libido does not get too involved. After all, love occupied very little space in the life of a person who had everything and who was torn between countless pleasures and impediments of passion and common sensuality. Aristides was more important, almost more indispensable, than that typical figure of a husband, José Moreira Matildes, who was a man in all his familial and social dimensionality.

"They say they love me. . . ." sang Rosamaria; and she struck poses in front of the mirror, which constituted almost the whole furniture of the room, except for the bed with bronze swans engraved on the headboard. This was the horrible Empire style of which the North had so few examples, except in the manor houses of Braga, and not in all of them. "Do you think I am pretty? I don't know why they love me. Look what a figure, Aristides! What a beanpole, what dark skin!" She laughed, enjoying the self-deprecation, which made her feel free and almost inhuman.

"Your eyes are something, Rosamaria! What a beautiful pair of eyes!"

AGUSTINA BESSA-LUÍS

"My eyes? Does anyone fall for a pair of eyes? Have you ever seen the eyes of a carp or of an opah? They are stuck in a disgusting white jelly. So are mine. Nothing is pretty, except in stories."

"Then, you are a story. . . ." Aristides sat on the rug and seemed enchanted or only amused at that little eleven-year-old girl who would not stop dancing and staring at the mirror with gestures that made her look ridiculous. That way vanity could not catch up with her; that was her trump, her last card—and her pride emerged unscathed from the trial, a terrible thing in the case of this child who was already molding the devilish character of the utterly indomitable woman she would become.

Translated by Francisco Cota Fagundes

"MOTHER, MOTHER, WHY HAVE YOU FORSAKEN ME?"

by

Natália Correia

NATÁLIA CORREIA

Like the protagonist of the short story translated here, Natália Correia is a native of the Azores (she was born on the island of St. Michael in 1923) and like her, she moved to the mainland for her education. She remained in Lisbon and embarked on dual literary and political careers that have combined to make her one of the most formidable Portuguese women of all time.

Correia's political career began early with a two-pronged resistance to the Salazar regime: as a participant in militant groups and as a writer determined to exercise the right to free expression. For the latter, she was censured and prosecuted. Her daring publication in 1966 of an anthology of erotic poetry earned her a three-year suspended sentence and anticipated the difficulties that were to be encountered by the authors of New Portuguese Letters *some years later. Not to be dissuaded, she went on writing books that were sure to be censored by the repressive regime. Her courageous tenacity reaped unexpected rewards after the Revolution of 1974: she was elected to Parliament as a Social Democrat and later, after a short absence from that body, returned as an independent. She continues to be one of the strongest, most lucid, and most conscience-driven voices on the Portuguese political scene.*

In a strictly literary sense, Natália Correia's career has been equally phenomenal. The author of nearly forty books, she has cultivated all genres and a wide range of themes: poetry, short fiction, the novel, theater, the political essay and diary, literary criticism. Since the Revolution, she has made a point of publishing the works previously condemned by the dictatorship along with her more recent work.

One of her country's leading feminists, she has also had a successful television program, Mátria, *a series of profiles of distinguished Portuguese women. "Mátria" is also the term that Natália Correia uses in speaking of a cherished theory: the notion that if humanity is to remain viable, it will have to redirect its energies from the male aggression that presently rules society* to the nurturing force normally associated with the female but equally conceivable within a male body. Natália Correia's work, literary and political, is of a piece. It is the expression of a strong-willed woman known both for her integrity and for her rebelliousness. While these characteristics may have been imparted to her originally by a liberal mother herself rebelling against the pious, conservative insular mentality of the Azores, they have developed self-consciously in a public persona who has tellingly asserted, "My cause is to combat the extinction of causes."

The short story included here in its entirety was published in A Ilha de Circe (Circe's Island, 1983). Like other stories in the collection, it is at once localized in its reflection of Azorean life and lore and universal. In it Correia—ever the social critic—ridicules the empty pedantry common in some strata of the Portuguese educational system. At the same time, she sets forth an ironic view of women's lot that resonates far beyond the story's insular context. In the story, an adolescent female half-consciously echoes her mother's developmental experience. Passion fruit is the symbolic link (and dividing line) between the two lives, a forbidden fruit that represents the fatalistic continuum between the mother's past and the daughter's present.

Works by Natália Correia

Poetry

Rio de Nuvens, *1947*
Poemas, *1955*
Dimensão Encontrada, *1957*
Passaporte, *1955*
Comunicação, *1959*
Cântico do País Emerso, *1961*
O Vinho e a Lira, *1966*
Mátria, *1968*
As Maçãs de Orestes, *1970*
A Mosca Iluminada, *1972*
O Anjo do Ocidente à Entrada do Feno, *1973*
Poemas a Rebate, *1975*

NATÁLIA CORREIA

Epístola aos Iamitas, *1976*
O Dilúvio e a Pomba, *1979*
O Armistício, *1985*
Sonetos Românticos, *1991*

Fiction

Anoiteceu no Bairro, *1946*
A Madona, *1968*
A Ilha de Circe, *1983*
Onde Está o Menino Jesus?, *1987*
As Núpcias, *1992*

Theater

O Progresso de Edipo, *1957*
O Homúnculo, *1965*
O Encoberto, *1969*
Erros Meus, Má Fortuna, Amor Ardente, *1981*
A Pécora, *1983*

Essays

Descobri que Era Europeia, *1951*
Poesia de Arte e Realismo Poético, *1958*
Uma Estátua para Heroides, *1974*
Somos Todos Hispanos, *1988*

Diaries

Não Percas a Rosa, *1978*

Literary Criticism and Anthologies

A Questão Académica de 1907, *1962*
Antologia da Poesia Erótica e Satírica, *1966*
Cantares Galego-Portugueses, *1970*
Trovas de D. Dinis, *1970*
A Mulher, *1973*
O Surrealismo na Poesia Portuguesa, *1973*
Antologia da Poesia Portuguesa no Período Barroco, *1982*
A Ilha de Sam Nunca, *1982*

"MOTHER, MOTHER, WHY HAVE YOU FORSAKEN ME?"

By eleven p.m., the lecturing architect had convinced a hundred people that logic had, finally, taken possession of architecture. And he concluded the proficient talk with a challenge that overwhelmed us:

"As I have demonstrated, even the normative flowering of modern architecture tells us that we are in the greatest epoch of human history."

The speaker summoned us to be conscious of an enormous responsibility: we were the generation chosen to carry humanity to glory. It was to lighten the weight that this dreadful distinction of our insignificance would assume in our individual solitudes that we agreed, on that very hot June night, that it was too early to go home to bed.

The professor, who was eminent in that modern academic democracy, refuge of worthless pedagogical artifice, suggested that we go to his house for refreshments.

Originally published as "Mãe, Mãe por que me abandonaste." In *A Ilha de Circe* (*Circe's Island*), by Natália Correia (Lisbon: Publicações Dom Quixote, 1983).

NATÁLIA CORREIA

It may be true that our philosophy professor wanted only, with that invitation, to have another opportunity to regale his students with the merits of his generative semantics. His insistence on our being at the lecture couldn't have been otherwise motivated. As we would see, even the most advanced architecture, hand in hand with linguistics, confirmed, in the exaggeration of surfaces, the adaptation to the . . .
". . . dreadful law of numbers," Pedro muttered in my ear. He was irritated by this disdain of the Master for sentiments and causes which gnawed at the depth of his being.
We went. A little while later, we found ourselves in his bachelor's apartment which, exemplifying the tyrannical law of surfaces, glistened with straight lines of metal, glass, and formica. The professor slipped into the kitchen to prepare the refreshments, leaving us with the only objects of his hospitality, shelves of books on transformational grammar and theories of abstract verbs. What a bore for anyone who wanted to escape the lecturer's linguistic stranglehold. Nothing to be done about it. The professor appeared with a carafe full of a thick yellow liquid which he poured into our glasses.
"Passion fruit juice," he said with a deliberate slowness. It seemed even intimidating when he offered me a glass with these words which seduced me with a disturbing familiarity:
"Passion fruit are abundant on your island." And the pointed tone in his voice of malicious complicity:
"They are also called torments."
Yes, they are also called torments!
Confess, old vulture, that it is not by accident that you soak that sly arrogance which springs from between your small withered legs in passion fruit juice while explaining that the use of mocking suffixes can induce one to homicide or asceticism.
No one drinks, no matter what it may be, just by chance. It is the guts and not the words that decide. Your guts demand the blood of my childhood yellowed by time. In them, I can perhaps decipher, like the ancient augurs, the mystery of a destiny which unites us.
With one finger jabbing the air, the professor now designates a new object of study. It is the interjective phrases with which Pedro attacks the philological impudence that confuses ascetics with murderers.

"MOTHER, MOTHER, WHY HAVE YOU FORSAKEN ME?"

The professor's didacticism flares:
"But look, my friend . . . The mocking suffix expresses the contempt of the world. . . . The ascetic kills it by turning his back on it. It is passive genocide. The active murderer destroys it in the victim on whom he feeds his loathing for humanity. But do not fear. Your ejaculatory inclination is peacefully religious. It does not allow any shade of despising suffix that may carry it to the narcissistic neurosis of monasticism or murder."

Caught in the mesh of the Master's inexhaustible rhetoric, Pedro protested in vain that he was an atheist.

But how can this be? We are no better than horses spurred by a swarm of words that obliges us to neigh. Is this language?

The suffocated voice of a girl, uterinely wounded by the chauvinistic prepotency of so much philological knowledge, shook off the torpor provoked by the professor's monologue:

"May I open a window? The newspapers say there hasn't been a June this hot in twenty years."

A good opportunity for the professor to insist:

"Another glass of passion fruit juice?"

Okay. Do you want me to drink my own blood? I accept.

My mother combs my hair. She tells me stories about the Tritons and sea nymphs which surround the island. Dogs and sea bitches who bark at the boats that come to bother the islanders. My mother sits down at the piano. From her delicate hands come threads of music which intertwine with the melody of the sea moving in time with the languor of the afternoon. Then she goes to the orchard to occupy herself with the passion fruit plants.

I spy on her through the window. Her eyes tenderly follow a branch which climbs through the trellis. She brings her mouth close to the livid violet flowers as if she could suck from their goblet shapes the potion of a martyred love. It is clear that she is bewitched by the passion fruit.

Ah, my mother's torments! I want to have them with you.

"Mama, give me a passion fruit!"

She enfolds me in her milky arms:

"No, my love. The passion fruit are not ours."

I scream. I scream louder inside. I taste blood.

"Maria da Estrela, you saw my mother born; tell me who the passion fruit belong to."

NATÁLIA CORREIA

The old maid put her toothless mouth next to my ear:
"I am going to tell you so you will leave me alone. But don't say anything to your mother. The passion fruit belong to the Doctor."
"Who is the Doctor?"
"Now . . . now. You weren't born yet."
"But what was there before I was born?"
"The same that will be after you die."
"And where do I go when I die?"
"I already told you, child. To the same place you came from."
Oh! Is that it? That is where the Doctor is.

Who could this inhabitant of the world of death be? This gluttonous ghost of the torments which my mother cultivated with a zeal that was a punishment for my usury of her caresses. I couldn't even imagine that in the life of that mother virginally portrayed in the Immaculate Mary, radiant among the other worm-eaten and discolored saints in the oratory, there might have passed the shadow of any man other than my father. And even he lived with her in chastity. It wasn't all that strange, because my mother was a silver-plated Virgin Mary. Looking at her porcelain features and sweet countenance, it was more than obvious that my father had touched that immaculately conceived body as much as Saint Joseph had the pure flesh of the Virgin Mary.

I had settled on this version of my birth after my grandmother had cured the nausea that made me vomit, secretly, for days.

It was like this:

My cousin Ermelinda, who already had small breasts on a small body ripened by twelve sensual years of tepid climate and salt sea air, armed herself to deflower my sainted ignorance of the mysteries which bring us into the world. She entered into repulsive details and I hated her because that filth sullied my mother, who, in her purity, was peerless.

How to expulse this venom with which that perverted Ermelinda had poisoned all of my thoughts? I tried to vomit it out. But it didn't come. No matter how hard I forced myself, even to the point of sweating, I couldn't manage to suppress a shiver when my mother braided my hair, ending that affec-

"MOTHER, MOTHER, WHY HAVE YOU FORSAKEN ME?"

tionate care with a flurry of kisses all over my cheeks. But she didn't notice anything. At that time, she was very busy with the passion fruit. She used to bring them home from the orchard in a basket and spilling them out on the dining room table, caressed them as if playing the piano. Then she wrapped them up in silk paper and put them in a wooden box in which they would travel to the continent. But how was this possible? We were surrounded by Tritons and sea nymphs who wouldn't let us leave the island and only the passion fruit were able to cross the sea? This was witchcraft. My mother was bewitched and the sorcerer was the Doctor who lived in the place we would go to when we died.

The picture that I formed of this despotic absentee was symbolically demon-like: horns, cloven hooves, forked tail, and all the rest that the horror of eternal sins paints for us as attributes of the devil. And to think that this dirty pig who fed on passion fruit was taking my bewitched mother as an obedient slave of his evil power. Could Ermelinda have been right when she told me those indecent things that my mother did so that I could be born?

I had to yank out that thorn that my cousin had stuck in a feeling that was my reason for living: the hidden fire of passion that I had for my mother; so absolute was it that the idea of not having her as a partner tormented me. None other was my acrimony for that Doctor with whom she played a mysterious game of passion fruit. But to believe that my mother was my father's partner in a filthy game which had engendered my life was going too far. And I had to force that sow Ermelinda to swallow the indecencies with which she dirtied my mother, because these weren't things you said about the Immaculate Conception which was my mother portrayed in the splendor of her purity.

I finally decided. Grandmother! It's true that at times she didn't make sense. But that was when she was mad and they came to look for her. She resisted, but they put her in a straitjacket. My mother cried but said there was nothing else that could be done. Now she was replaced by that sarcastic queen who, in the dimness of her room, conversed with invisible people. At these times she said the most beautiful things. And the more that Maria da Estrela said, when I repeated those things to her, that Grandmother, poor thing, wasn't right in the

NATÁLIA CORREIA

head, I thought that those things, being so beautiful, had to be true.

I went to see her in her room, which was a bazaar of musty and extravagant objects. Of these, the one that made the greatest impression on me was an old dressmaker's mannequin. It had a yellow belt and wavy bandoleer from which hung a small wedge of wood, a gray leather apron, and in the place where the lapel ought to be a ribbon with green borders from which hung a whistle and a little golden hatchet. My grandmother looked so comical playing up to that perforated mannequin she called Prince Sublime. I had no idea I would incur her wrath by asking for those trinkets to dress up in. Good Lord, what did you say! Curses flying, she terrified me with the threat that I was going to be stabbed mercilessly. This was what happened to those who betrayed the great mysteries that I wanted to ridicule in impious foolishness and that was an insult to Saint Tibaldo, who had died a sainted death covered with pus and ulcers and therefore was the patron saint of coal miners.

Sweating and terrified, I ran for Maria da Estrela and hid behind her skirt from the dread of the dagger thrown by my grandmother's insults, which I was sure I saw flying behind me.

"The dagger . . . I saw the dagger to kill me."

"What dagger, child?"

"Grandmother said I was going to be knifed to death because I asked her for the mannequin's apron and ribbon to play dress up in."

She grunted indifferently. But my outburst of tears called forth the prosaic maternal instinct with which she alleviated the neglect of my own mother's lyrical, dreamy maternity.

She wiped away my tears with her apron and set about to calm me down:

"Don't be afraid. The dagger only exists in her crazy head. But don't ask her again for the mannequin's ornaments. That's asking for trouble. They belonged to your grandfather, who had a mean streak in him, and no one can tell me he didn't drive her crazy. Scoundrels. Evil people who kill kings to subject us to these republics in which there is neither shame nor respect for anyone. I'm from the days of the monarchy; that really was respect."

I went to find my grandmother in her habitual spot: a large

"MOTHER, MOTHER, WHY HAVE YOU FORSAKEN ME?"

old chair covered with threadbare silk; we didn't have money in that house to restore the decrepit furniture. She had at hand on a little table gold, silver, and amber snuff boxes along with religious articles, medicines, and whistles to use according to her whims. The whistles were to summon Maria da Estrela, who, biting her tongue, acquiesced to this shrill form of summons to fulfill obsolete orders such as: "Have the horses harnessed and the carriage brought around. I am going out." It was for that departure, whose destination she guarded like a secret, to which we, mere guests in her delirious universe, were not privy, that bundles, many bundles, began to pile up in every corner of her room.

"Pst!" she said when she saw me, despite the fact that I had crept in on tiptoes. "Let me hear what they are saying."

She seemed to be satisfied with what her immaterial interlocutors had said, because, after stretching the curls of wrinkles which stuck to her bony face into a knowing smile, she inhaled a good pinch of snuff.

Seeing that she was in a good mood encouraged me to ask her:
"Who are you talking to, Grandmother?"
"The angels, don't you see?"
"No; I don't see."
"Of course. How are you supposed to see them if you're blinded by so many lies?!"
"You're right, Grandmother. Cousin Ermelinda lied to me. She told me my mother did awful things with my father so that I could be born."

Her sunken eyes flashed in their skeletal sockets.

"That worm of a cousin of yours dares to slander the Virgin Mary? Listen, child, men are good for nothing. Not even to make children. Read the Bible. Saint Joseph became wild with rage when he saw that his chaste woman was going to have a child that couldn't be his. Because when he wanted to do those nauseating things with her that your damned cousin said your father did with your mother, the Blessed among women refused him, saying that only the Holy Spirit could enter her flesh like a ray of sunshine through a window. But the angel didn't allow the jealousy of a carpenter to dishonor the Rose of Jericho with abominable suspicions. He appeared to Saint Joseph and explained to him that it was a heavenly mystery that he didn't expect a laborer from Galilee to understand. And he remained in his humble and obscure place. It even seems that he disappeared because they say nothing about him in the wedding of Cana nor in the departure for Capernaum. He was like your father who was a good for nothing. And God save us from the plague which isn't needed here to make children because the Divine Holy Spirit takes charge of that service."

This pretentious interpretation of the matrimonial insignificance of Mary's husband, not unlike the heretical perversions of my mean-spirited grandfather who died before I was born, had a soothing effect on me. Not being able to contain my intense happiness, given how deep and dark my sorrow had been, I told Maria da Estrela, whose eyes widened when I interrupted the dishwashing with this joyous blasphemy:

"I am very happy. My father is like Saint Joseph. He disappeared like him and I am the daughter of my mother and the Holy Spirit."

The old servant put her hands on her hips and shaking her gray head went beyond the bounds of politeness in deploring the insolence with which I insulted the Gospel Saints.

"Enough! I bet it was your grandmother who put that damned idea in your head. That nutty old woman may drive you crazy yet. Now she wants to offend the Sainted Father, comparing him with your father who is off in Brazil doing God only knows what! Those are your grandfather's crazy ideas. He was a Jacobin, and his poor wife who was born into the good religion became unhinged and, in matters of faith, confuses one thing with another."

I stubbornly withstood her rosary and holy water reasoning which I found hateful since it gave new encouragement to my torments.

"You can't deny that Saint Joseph disappeared just like my father."

"And so what? He went to heaven."

"My father went to Brazil. Isn't that the same?"

"Child, don't annoy me. Oh, if it weren't for your dear little mother who I carried in my arms and who needs me because she's got her head in the clouds and because someone in this madhouse has to keep her wits about her . . . How are heaven and Brazil the same? Come here!"

"MOTHER, MOTHER, WHY HAVE YOU FORSAKEN ME?"

She took me energetically by the hand, her stiff legs reeling under her long full skirt, took me into the living room, and pointed at the picture of my father, chubby-faced and smiling brightly, that was hanging on the wall above the straw-stuffed sofa.

"Do you think he has the face of Saint Joseph?"

I shrugged my shoulders.

"I never saw Saint Joseph."

"If only you could. The saints only appear to people who are in the grace of God. And you go around bedevilled with this madness of confusing the Glorious Virgin's husband with your father who was a drunk. There was no end to his drunkenness and carousing. That's why he ruined the greenhouse business. And if he hadn't fled to Brazil to escape the bill collectors, squandering your grandmother's meager possessions, a few small pieces of property, she wouldn't be living in poverty now. This is the truth, and if you turn around and say that your harebrained father is exactly the same as the Sainted Father of the Sacred Family, I will ask the priest to give you forty Our Fathers to say as an act of contrition for the demons that torment your brain."

If the poor old woman suspected the firmness with which I denied her contention of Saint Joseph's immunity to the sacrilegious resemblance with my father the sinner, she would have feared for the damnation of my soul. So I wouldn't have to deal with her anymore, I outwardly agreed with her but secretly held on to my own view of things. So much so that if my father was drunk like she said, this was no reason for him not to be like Saint Joseph, since the priest also drank wine at mass.

My father settled into the carnally innocuous figure of a reputed father; my mother, unsullied by Ermelinda's indecent calumnies, returned intact to the fanaticism of my love. It gave me reason to hate the man, far away on the continent, who performed witchcraft with passion fruit. A soul of the devil who tempted my mother to sacrifice me to Satan.

What could there be in common between those arts of the devil and this stylistic tripod at the top of which the professor, who also feasts on my childhood torments, coiled like the python, inhaling the vapors of our voices, predicts good and bad luck, even suicide?

NATÁLIA CORREIA

The person who is the object of this last prediction is an unfortunate young girl in whose disheartening lack of attractions any fortuneteller would easily foresee a fate of painful rejection in romantic relationships. Disregarding other non-linguistic evidence, the professor would have us believe that the girl's ugly submissiveness is the psychosomatic effect of her muted voice. And from that he draws dark conclusions.

"What? Do you think I'm going to commit suicide, Professor?"

"Maybe. If you manage to raise the vocalic potential, your language moves away from the frontier of shadows. And, thus, you are saved."

I can't take any more. I fidget in my chair. Why didn't I escape like Pedro and the others who got away from this drudgery, excusing themselves because of the heat, which becomes more oppressive by the minute? What fluid evil binds me to this man who up until now only distinguished himself from the other professors by being a little more boring in selling us his science? Science of the snake, as one can see in the stupid anguished eyes of the student in whom he planted the seed of suicide.

With the departure of Pedro and the other students, the Master's audience was reduced to the girl who, if she isn't careful with her philology, may still end up stretched out from an overdose of barbiturates, a young man obsessed with leading student strikes, and me. Myself, stupifyingly held prisoner by a sick-natured fascination that I can't quite put my finger on. Or rather, that I don't want to understand. But that I distrust. And he provokes it by leading my spirit to that obscure point I want to avoid with the same revulsion with which I refuse to drink the passion fruit juice.

It is impossible to escape him. He notices that I haven't touched the drink.

"You don't like passion fruit juice?"

"No." And I furiously restrain myself from saying: "They are torments."

"I thought you would like it. I ate passion fruit for the first time on your island. And I acquired a taste for it. I went there with a student group. I tearfully sang the fado of Coimbra. A success! What beautiful women! One of them sticks in my mind.

"MOTHER, MOTHER, WHY HAVE YOU FORSAKEN ME?"

What a time that was! You weren't born yet. . . ."
He is lost in an emotional state that appears dredged up to invite me to follow it. And I allow myself to be guided by those gropings in the darkness of pent-up feelings that are opening the roads to the past, until they explode in a great feeling of despair from my childhood.

My mother is seated in a straight-backed chair; below her is the trellis of fruit that hides the evil of the man who passed through here before I was born. She has her hands flattened in her lap, the expression on her face frozen in a kind of pain which she seems to guard jealously; not wanting to lose it, she surrenders to it and remains immobile.

Mother, who makes you suffer so? Ah, it is that monstrous all-powerful one with the passion fruit, which you deny me because they belong to him, and only to him, like your soul.

I move away, enraged, from the window through which I spy on the anguish that robs her of the absoluteness of my love. And I cannot help crying, making desperate attempts not to be heard.

Maria da Estrela calls me for a snack. Choking back my tears, I tell her I can't go on anymore. I want to die.

"Good Lord, child! Who hurt you?"
"The Doctor."
"Which Doctor?"
"The one with the passion fruit."
"Good Lord. That was before you were born."
"But what was there before I was born?"
"The world of the soul, where you will go when you die."

Is that it? Then I have to die in order to find out who that evil one is who steals my mother's love from me?

Who could tell me? Not Maria da Estrela, who told me to be sensible when my afflictions transcended the succor of her tenderness, so ordinary and very practical. My mother, never. Just thinking that she could have even an inkling of my disrespectful curiosity about a man with whom she had mysterious relations made me shiver. There remained only Grandmother, who spoke with the dead and should know if I had to join them in order to face my enemy.

"Grandmother!"

She resents my calling her that and clarifies the situation with great dignity:

NATÁLIA CORREIA

"I am not your grandmother. Those people lied to you. I am of the noble race that came to populate this island and I live according to the law of the nobleman, as did my ancestors."

I submitted to her indignation, which was partly justified by the lineage she had inherited at birth, as Maria da Estrela remembered when she began to fret over the sad end of a woman of such noble descent. And I went right to the heart of the matter to find out once and for all:

"Is it true you talk to the dead?"

She paled in offended amazement at my uncertainty about her familiarity with those from the other side of the grave.

"You dare to doubt it?"

"I don't doubt it. Ask them who the Doctor is. If they tell you who he is, then I wouldn't have to die, right?"

"I don't have to ask. I know who the Doctor is. If you want to come with me, I'll take you to him."

"But he is on the continent where they send the passion fruit. It is where the dead are. We have to cross the ocean."

"That's a lie. They only tell you lies. Poor thing. They feed you sacrilege. Let's go."

And we went.

I approach the terrible consequence of my anxiety by penetrating the world of shadows where a horrendous being traded understandings with my mother that blinded me with jealousy.

In the burning lucidity of insanity, which, to satisfy its own designs, tricks the most attentive guardians, Grandmother escaped from the house with me in tow, mindful of her precautions not to get caught. In a black silk cloak dotted with glass beads fluttering over her shoulders, which bounced up and down in the frenetic vivacity of the trip, she took me through streets where the brownish sun dimmed the contrast between the whitewashed buildings and the blackness of the basalt underfoot. We arrived at the church square. She stopped suddenly. Her wild eyes surveyed the forms that sluggishly dotted the square. She fixed her sight finally on a row of cars parked among some arches and along one side of the stairway that wound around the church. That must have been the object of her goggle-eyed search because she took off on her skeletal legs, almost crushing my hand in her grip, reached the line of old jalopies, and

"MOTHER, MOTHER, WHY HAVE YOU FORSAKEN ME?"

resolutely got into one of them. The enthusiasm with which she pulled me into the car startled me. I had a sneaking suspicion that she was going to get me into trouble.

"We won't take a lot of time, will we, Grandmother?"

"No," she said with a smiling quickness which, in a way, relaxed me, and ordered the driver to take us to the Caves. The driver appraised the solemnly comical face and dated clothes of his customer through the rear-view mirror. He would have to have concluded that he was transporting one of the odd old ladies who in that land reluctant to embrace change exorcized it by clinging to old ways and clothing. To the driver's credit, he didn't bat an eye at having picked up such an archaic fare as Grandmother. She was always completely convincing in appearing to be perfectly in her right mind, so that when she felt the explosion of dementia coming on, that appearance managed to keep her from being carried off to the funny farm. She was in that precautionary state, thwarting the wardens of her liberty, when, with majestic serenity, she told the driver to go to the Caves.

In a little while, the car climbed the road winding among woods and fields. The gyrations made me dizzy and the giddiness spread to my feelings, which oscillated between the safe impulse to go home and the desire, chilling and therefore all the more seductive, of seeing in flesh and blood the apparition of my jealous nightmares. Vacillating between these two attractions, which grew in competition with the car's rocking, made me whimper.

And she was sarcastically disdainful of my cowardice in the face of the great perverseness of the meeting that she was going to provide for me:

"Why are you crying, child? Don't you want to meet the Doctor?"

The trip progressed far away from my house, where I imagined my distraught mother looking for me in every corner and pleading, consumed with pain, that they bring back her darling daughter. Or maybe not. She might not have even noticed my absence in that sleepwalking state of hers induced by the narcotic of those damned passion fruit. This thought cooled the remorse of alarming my mother with my escape, reviving the hatred for the man who was the unearthly personification of all that could rob me of my mother's love. Carried away by the very real possibility that I was going to remedy that situation one way or another, I clenched my teeth to hold back the nausea provoked by the car's jerking winding through woods, pastures, and hydrangea hedges which bulged in opulent blue along both sides of the road. Suddenly, at the bottom of a hill, light split open the sky like a solar twinge in the fitful climate, then flashed, reflected in a large swamp. But then it softened in the picturesque space of a row of houses, finally damning itself in a livid place scarred with whitish holed rocks that blew nauseous smoke. There was something hellish about that place of boiling sulfur. There, I thought, was the residence of damned souls where I figured the venomous manipulator who had poisoned my mother's thoughts lived.

It was there that Grandmother, joyfully screaming, ordered the car to stop. We got out. She thrust her hand in mine, which trembled under the pressure of her bony fingers, and leaping a short distance, she began to dance in a circle around open holes in the ground which exhaled fetid vapors and frightful heat. I had the sensation that the stench of rotten things which tortured me stimulated her to look for more atrocious evidence of the demon's abode. I wasn't fooled. With gloomy nimbleness she climbed some stairs and forced me next to a large puddle which snarled, erupting with frightening noises into torrents of seething water; and captivated by an intention which I suddenly realized was dreadful, she exclaimed:

"Here is the caldron of hell."

Born of a silent terror, my instinct of self-preservation was stronger than the tenacious energy with which she grasped my hand. I broke loose, and running for the top of the stairs, began screaming for my mother at the top of my lungs. She came toward me. Her eyes flashed with a gloomy joy. She grabbed me by the arm and dragged me toward the edge of the caldron, her hands held fast on my shoulders in a bloodthirsty attempt to throw me into the depths of that well of rumbles and infernal seething. I was struggling among these horrors, screaming loud enough to wake the dead, when I felt myself caught up in the driver's strong arms. The man deduced, at last, from my frenzied shouting, the dangers of dementia in the old woman whom he had mistaken for a harmless old lady.

"MOTHER, MOTHER, WHY HAVE YOU FORSAKEN ME?"

Rescued from the homicidal fury of my grandmother, I plunged into a cloud of fever and tears. I remember my mother, her face convulsed, bent over, weeping, on the bed in which I dozed in the torpor that followed the fits of delirium.

Grandmother went to the asylum. She only came out once, on a morning whipped by wild rain: nature hastening the funeral dispatches from the land of the dead for that woman so dementedly disturbing to the peaceful sanity of the living.

The shock that put me on the brink of a mental breakdown dispersed the phantasmagoria compounded by my jealousy. Only one bitter feeling remained; an uneasiness that always ate at my heart: that my mother, as if fulfilling a blessed devotion, packed up the passion fruit that went to Lisbon.

And the time came for me to leave also.

"In a small land, there is limited space for study."

My uncle said this at my graduation party when I graduated from high school with honors. Amid the food and festivities, the conversation turned to whether or not I should go to the university. And since there wasn't a man in the house to make decisions about important family matters, it was my uncle who, in such matters, had the final say. Now the university was a thorn in his side, reminding him of a fate that had diverted him from becoming a doctor, his great vocation. Because of the charms of an erotically excessive widow who consumed him at age seventeen, and so that he would not remain irremediably tubercular, as he had sworn that this would be his ultra-romantic end if he did not marry her, my grandmother consented to his curing himself in the conjugal juice of that fat hen. Seeing the vulnerable boy ravaged by the widow's debauched talons drove my grandmother crazy. Maria da Estrela had her own view of the situation, and not being objective when it came to my mean-spirited grandfather, blamed him for the mental darkness of that poor woman.

Tiresomely cured by the bad marriage that had killed his inclination for medicine, my uncle didn't miss a chance to blame the woman who had sucked the blood out of his desired career, recommending the university as the only way of evading the island's meanness. It was on this resentful note that he paternally offered to defray part of the expense of my installation in Lisbon; he would use some of the money left to us by Grandmother, who was now with her dead beneath the earth in the Saint Joachim cemetery.

Thus was removed my mother's feeble argument in opposition to my going to study in Lisbon, if that was what I wanted. Desire mixed with sadness at leaving her in her fragile state. But I was already at the stage of being unsettled by the insular fatality of leaving that presents itself to some in the form of economic opportunity and to others—this was my case—in the promise of great and exciting things that happen on the other side of the ocean. This appeal was more powerful than the pain of separating myself from that mother so sweetly doomed to always being abandoned. By my father. Now by me. And in another time . . . in another time by someone who had left a hypnotic fluid in the passion fruit plants that languished in the orchard. Dark figure of the jealous imagination of my youth. Under lock and key in the hiding place where I shut the horror of having been almost consumed in the flames of hell where I wished to go to defy her.

And so, that having been the situation, on this steamy night of insupportable heat, the professor, overheated by linguistic weight, awakens those discordant reminiscences. He wrings them from their lethargy, in the mellifluous way he stares at me, each time pausing in the tide of his torrential mastery, sipping a bit of the passion fruit juice, savoring the taste as if getting ready, afterward, to eat my heart. I must be crazy attributing to this bore a lugubrious greatness which lends him an air of dark seduction. Maria da Estrela was right when she said to me: "With that nonsense, you'll end up crazy like your grandmother."

I try to hide from these head games and force myself to follow the conversation, which is getting heated. The professor just caught the budding revolutionary red-handed in his use of the article.

"If you had said, 'they are combat methods,' the omission of the small morpheme would indicate the partitive, democratic meaning of your ideas. But you said, 'they are *the* methods of combat.' And so that there could be no doubt, you emphasized the article in an expressly despotic incision. Now the use and the unmistakable accentuation betray a strong totalitarian inclination. Patience, your insurrectionist passion only aims at splitting with the established order to implant a more repressive regime."

Wiping off sweat with the side of his hand, the fervor of indignation foaming down his throat and forehead, my classmate chokes on unfinished protests. Then what about Vaneigem? What about Bendit and the group of May 1968? Along with them he is against all the fascist mob on the right and the left.

The professor tries to calm him down. Yes, but . . . yes, but . . . But, damn it, all is not lost. It is only a question of strengthening by cutting off the tyrannical little morpheme and the democratic generosity will gush forth from the depths in which the subjugated use of the article wants to keep it prisoner.

The end of this journey was softened with the honeyed tone of an apostolate:

"My children, in good and true linguistics I say to thee, when men finally see that it is language that forms thought, then many crimes will be avoided."

The evangelicalism in which the professor velvetizes his *dixit* piques my friend who, calling a spade a spade, explodes in an ironical retort:

"The best thing for us is to remain mute. There is no vocabulary more incisive to awaken the sleeping murderer."

With irritated delicacy, the Master conjures up out of the student's sarcastic fierceness an image that delights him:

"Yes . . . yes. The giddiness of our civilization imposes an economy of words. The disciplined conciseness of laconism. And in the end . . . silence." In a hasty transition, as if he had just resolved the mystery of Paradise Lost: "That's it. . . . That's it. Language seeks the silence which sinfully fell, like man, from paradise."

Excited by the exaltation of this discovery, he refills the glasses with passion fruit juice. He prepares to toast his theoretical triumph, paradisical silence. But no one joins him. I draw back with a negative gesture when he urges me to raise the drink to my mouth. The others are about to leave. My classmate is livid for having to carry the burden of that totalitarianism without acting against the author of such a defaming verdict. The girl, sheltered by the virile strength of the revolutionary, hides from the macabre blasts of language that augur her suicide.

"It's time to be going," says the young man with undisguised

haste to put distance between himself and the Master before he punches that abusive science. And he assumes that I, too, am eager to find myself free of that insidious bore: Are you coming?
How? I want to. But I can't. The professor holds me in a despotic serenity that immobilizes my will to leave.
"I'm staying a while."
They leave. The slamming of the door as it closes is the last sound from a world in which I would be laughing at the magic farce that binds me to this repulsive man.
Well, then, Doctor, was this our meeting? I observe him.
He sits down next to me on the vomit-colored sofa. Good Lord, what butterflies in my stomach! Could I have vomited all of this? this scene? His knees almost touch mine. . . . He is very tiny. Toadlike. The hypnotic contention on his face sharpens his roving eyes. Now they stare at the opening of my blouse, which reveals the emerging cleavage of my breasts. His mouth, rough with chapped lips, has hardened bits of saliva compressed in the corners. How disgusting! Then he opens it, and the jaggedness of his yellowed gaping teeth makes him look like an evil child. His very high forehead arches up to a hump where his hair breaks out, plastered down by sweat in shiny strands. The sunken chest heaves up in a tumultuous gasping for breath which, in a corner of my memory, grows in roars of infernal agitation. And I, passionately passive, falling headlong into the fiery flames of his desire. What heat! Undress me, Doctor. Isn't that the science of your linguistics? Stripping souls bare until they are completely naked, free of the words that engendered their free will. Pure, in the blissful inexpression of wanting nothing. Do you want me to drink some passion fruit juice? I take hold of the cup that is sitting on the table within my reach. I take a sip. Do you want me to savor this potion of blood and ashes? It is good. It tastes like the night. A night sweetly draining from a milky moon, tumescent and white like the breast my mother gave me to nurse from. I am ready, Doctor. Dutifully bewitched to abandon the tremulous flower of my virginity to your sword of fire.
He begins to unbutton my blouse. A dark cloud covers the milky moon.
Mother, mother, why have you forsaken me?

Translated by Kim Marinus

solitude and with the nobility of their efforts to reach beyond it with dignity. The story appeared in the collection Estação Morta *(*Off Season, *1980).*

Works by Maria Ondina Braga

Eu Vim Para Ver a Terra, *1965*
A China Fica ao Lado, *1968*
Estátua de Sal, *1969*
Amor e Morte, *1970*
Os Rostos de Jano, *1973*
A Revolta das Palavras, *1975*
A Personagem, *1978*
Mulheres Escritoras, *1980*
Estação Morta, *1980*
O Homem da Ilha e Outros Contos, *1982*
A Casa Suspensa, *1982*
Angústia em Pequim, *1984*
Lua de Sangue, *1986*
Nocturno em Macau, *1991*

THE WOMAN WHO WANTED TO DIE

That morning, rather late, she decided: it was time. She was seventy-nine years old, her heart exhausted, her soul detached. She stood up on sagging legs, her eyesight clouded, dressed herself with difficulty, and began to put her things in order. First of all her letters: letters spoke like people: those of her husband before their marriage, those of her daughter who had vanished into the world. She took them from the chest of drawers, piled them up, tied them together with string, the knot running through her blighted fingers. Then, the photographs: the one of her wedding, the one of Julia six months old, sitting on top of a table in her beribboned little smock, the one of her godmother Rufina, the one of her godson laid out and surrounded by flowers. *Guide to Heaven*—her first communion book. A necklace of glass beads (Julia's? her own when she was young?). She had lived so long that now she was mixing up her own life

---

Originally published as "A Mulher que Queria Morrer." In *Estação Morta* (*Off Season*), by Maria Ondina Braga (Lisbon: Vega, 1980).

THE WOMAN WHO WANTED TO DIE

with that of her daughter. For example, at times she would think: that pink sateen dress . . . And she would see Julia before the mirror, her epaulettes, her neck so very white as it emerged from the ornate neckline. How nice she looked in it. . . . How nice I looked in it. . . . She must have died, Julia, otherwise she would have written. How could she *not* have mixed them up? The dead live again in the living. An empty bottle of perfume: so pure the scent still lingered in the vial, though it had gone dry years ago. That she remembered well: a gift from her man on their first anniversary. A clothing store salesclerk, her João. They had met at a Chamber of Commerce dance. A fan of threadbare silk. Julia's first slippers, her first braid. A small bamboo tray. A raffia basket. She piled it all together on the chest of drawers.

Then, in the kitchen, she had a sudden dizzy spell, sat down on a stool, and leaned her head on the sink. My God, not right now . . . Alone like this, no! Regaining her breath, she put some water on for tea. She looked out the small window. The sun was climbing. One could sense the first days of spring. And she counted her "treasures" on her fingers: three, four, six. And the rest? Well, the rest, bah, old bottles, tattered rags, shards, fragments. She took off her slippers and with some difficulty put on her shoes; her swollen feet were hard to squeeze in; she couldn't tighten the straps. She looked around: the parlor, the kitchen. She never said "room," but always "parlor," just like back home where she came from. In the parlor of her childhood had slept her parents; in that of her womanhood, she and her husband; Julia in the alcove. Here, however, there was no alcove, and she had sold the rattan sofa shortly after her husband's death. She straightened the blankets, passed a dust cloth over the sparse furniture, sighed. If her Julia had not . . . died? it was on her she would be relying at this moment. Julia—attentive, zealous, quick. What a comfort. She wouldn't have to be gathering together the things she valued. Julia would keep them, just the same as if they were remaining in her own hands.

She leaned back, gathering strength for the journey. She had hardly any neighbors, she lived in that hole in the ground, to tell the truth, she didn't get along with anyone. And really, she wasn't from here. She had come after Julia, who had then taken off, going even further, carried on by the winds of a greedy and fatal destiny. She combed out her thin hair. A presence. Someone unknown but friendly. Did such people still exist? The hospital, no. Doctors, nurses, out of the question. She wasn't ill, just fed up, tired, worn to the bone. In any case, she couldn't stay there all day long. On hands and knees, if need be, she had to get out, to meet people—anyone.

The cobbled way rose steeply, she had to climb clinging to the walls, she stopped many times, yet she never thought of giving up. She walked for what seemed like hours. Finally, the square and the arcades. She leaned against one of the pillars, gasping. Busy creatures passed before her, groups of chatterers, children holding their mothers' hands, knapsacks on their backs, lonely men, as well, glancing at wristwatches, hailing taxis. They tripped over her, coming within a hair of knocking her to the ground. It was enough to drive you mad, the noise of the cars and the motorbikes. She looked for her usual corner. She spoke to herself: "Cremilde, don't get discouraged. God is great. Santa Philomena. The soul of Julia, if she's already there . . ." Her chest hurt and she could scarcely lift her arms to brush back the thin wisps of hair from her eyes.

A half hour passed, perhaps more, and traffic doubled. It was like the roaring of the sea. She was filled with a kind of contentment at having been able to walk so far and reach the square. All week she hadn't come for lack of courage. Now she began to remember familiar faces: those of the girls from the high school. A girl—a student? a teacher?—used to place a silver coin silently in her pocket. A slip of a girl, a pretty thing, always alone. What if she were to appear right now? And why not? The truth is other people give me money, but none with that discreet manner, almost ashamed. She blushed: to hold out her hand to charity . . . No, that no. They saw her under the arches, bent over, badly dressed, and they wanted to help her: that's all: quite simple. Aha, if her João had foreseen the end she would come to . . . Her João. The bottle of perfume. She had never used it, but had emptied it all into the coffin. The visits of condolence: look, fragrant like the bodies of saints . . . Julia, at thirteen, fainting away, a woman for the first time. Her godmother.

If only the quiet girl of the timid offering could be at her side. But what if she didn't come? Especially on this day of greatest

THE WOMAN WHO WANTED TO DIE

need? My God, make her come! There's no one else I can count on. I'll wait all day, all day long. Poor you, Cremilde, suffer with patience. Someone who has lived seventy-nine years like you surely can wait one more hour. That frail young girl, shy, silent. She would stop, open her purse, walk toward her, head down, slip five escudos into the pocket of her threadbare overcoat. Once she had gone on, even if there was nothing else, Cremilde would head for home. Those five escudos profitted her as if they were blessed. She regretted exchanging them for a couple of rolls and an apple.

Amelia followed her usual path across the square to the bus stop for the 27, which would take her to the Young Women's Residence. Typist at an insurance company, she finished work at six o'clock. She was twenty-five and had come from the countryside in search of work seven years earlier. In search of work and to free herself from the family environment. Her father, the owner of a workshop, had made a second marriage to a widow of some means and no manners: she would stand at the front door barefoot, gossiping, gesticulating, yelling, embarrassing her step-daughter no end.

Amelia. Her mother had died when she was about five. She could remember her pallid face, her crossed hands with their purple fingernails, and the hearse, its horses with their black felt trappings, her grandmother holding her in her arms and taking her to the window so she could watch her depart forever in the sumptuous carriage. Her grandmother. A second mother. If the grandmother hadn't departed as well, perhaps her father would never have married again. Perhaps you, Amelia, would now be back home, working—and why not?—in the office of the small workshop. There, at least, no one would laugh at your Guimarães accent: "flow-ah" instead of "floor," "mow-ah" instead of "more." As long as her grandmother was alive, her father had never dared receive that woman within his doors: a sloven who spoke and laughed too loud, used curse words, received clients in a blouse faded under the armpits, her skirt askew, a rat's nest on top. But for all that, Amelia, you feel no more comfortable in Lisbon. In the residence, the girl with whom you share a room drinks, takes drugs, startles you in the middle of the night with her bellowing and retching. And friends, you can't pride yourself on having friends: your temperament, drawn within yourself, distrustful of everyone. Ah, what yearning for the old days, the dusty smell of the wool, of the twine, of the burlap in the textile shop below the house. Nostalgia even for that day of prayers and mourning, and the fantastical coach, and the clip-clop of the horses' hooves. Nostalgia for everything from there, except for the stepmother, who, without being bad, my God, how unpleasant.

She was leaving the luggage shop where she had gone for a repair, when she came across the poor lady. It had been wicked long since she had seen her. And why did she give her anything? Because she was old and reminded her of her grandmother? Or out of a disguised, circuitous self-love? Or the pleasure of feeling useful? A life without value: typing away for hours on end, earning little, taking refuge in a corner of that violated room, saving up for a dress, a pair of shoes, suspicious of people . . .

There was the old lady, huddled up under an arch. Amelia stopped beside her, opened her purse, felt someone pulling at her sleeve. It was the old lady, Cremilde, suddenly looking dreadful, pleading with her:

"Ah, young lady, I'm not feeling well. Please . . . Help me. If you could get me home . . . It's close by. Ah, if only you could . . ."

The girl hesitated. Who knew who that little old lady was! She was steadying herself on her. With eyes shut and lips pressed tight, like someone holding in a violent pain, and still hanging on to her sleeve, the old lady spoke, through clenched teeth, of dizziness, of feeling sick, but don't worry about it, no, it would be enough to accompany her to over there, close by, at the end of the Calçada dos Navegantes. For the love of God, for her own good fortune.

And, to her own surprise, Amelia saw herself take the poor woman's arm in her own, giving her a little pat on the shoulder and stammering some words of consolation: yes, she would accompany her. She should rest her mind. It would be no problem. It would make no difference whether she got back to the residence at seven or at nine. And they set off. The street was a back-breaker. While adjusting her step to that of the poor old woman, who was weighing heavily on her right arm, hunching over, intent on her steps, Amelia reflected on what she was doing. Charity? But what's all this about charity in a frivolous and egotistical world such as that of Lisbon? No, there was no room

THE WOMAN WHO WANTED TO DIE

for charity here. Furthermore, whom could one trust, nowadays, especially in the big cities? Couldn't the old woman be leading her on, in the pay of others? A voice inside her, warning her: "Better don't go. It's dangerous. . . ." Besides, it was strange how quickly the poor woman had stopped panting, stopped moaning. Was it all for show? Now she seemed almost normal to her, with a suspicious-looking hope gleaming in her half-closed little eyes. And Amelia held back. But the other, lifting her head of white hair, threw her an imploring, humble look: "You don't want to come, do you?" The girl smiled a sickly smile and continued on. She had been raised hearing about charity, kindness, compassion, but nowadays one didn't dare to even utter such words for fear that someone might laugh in one's face. O.K., everything had its time and its place. Before, in the northern town where she was born, these were called virtues, qualities worth cultivating. But here, in the capital, now, how they echoed of sanctimoniousness and backwardness. If I were to tell them, tomorrow, at work, that I took a sick old lady home, what would they all say? A naive girl is what they would call me: on every street there are people faking illness and poverty. . . . Naive and foolish: the old woman could belong to some gang of thieves. "Why get yourself involved in the whole thing? Call Emergency, 115, and that's that!" Little would they know that that had been the first idea that occurred to her. And, yet, there she was, going along the street, giving her arm to the beggar, whom she didn't know, to whom she hadn't ever even spoken, moved by her appeal—and, worst of all, without knowing what had led her to such an act. Yes, for "charity" no longer said anything to her. She lived alone, sad, without affection, exploited by her boss, by the landlady, by her own roommate.

The old woman took a few slower steps and stopped for breath. Amelia asked:

"What is your name?"

"Cremilde, at your service."

She found the "at your service" funny—what an old-fashioned way of talking! Especially as there were no servants anymore . . . Then she noticed how at ease Cremilde was, the promptness of her response, her cheerfulness almost. (Where, in the end, was that sickness, that dizziness?) All her life she had heard that the poor were cunning. . . . And yet she felt her body

MARIA ONDINA BRAGA

trembling and a chill coming from her: from the snow of her hair? from the weak breath of her toothless mouth?—something that grieved her on this warm late afternoon in April.

Arriving at the tiny house half in ruins next to a walled yard, Cremilde began to rub herself like a cat against the latchless door, which swung inward, revealing two steps and, at the bottom, a vast, uncomfortable basement room with a narrow bed, a trunk, a chest of drawers, a broken caned-bottom chair. The only room—Cremilde informed her—beside the kitchen. Through the window, close to the low ceiling, entered the last light of day. Cremilde lit the kerosene lamp and, with the pillow from the bed, improvised a seat for Amelia on the broken chair. Then she went to boil some water for a nice cup of tea. Amelia followed her. The kitchen was roofed with naked tiles and the stove was a tripod over coals. All along, the old woman was unrolling her life: the husband, such a great friend, had left her a widow at twenty-eight, she had not wanted another, there was no other like him; the daughter, who went to work in America, she hadn't heard from her in close to thirty years. She became silent. Amelia imagined her crying inside—the exhausted tears of old age and of waiting and hoping without hope. But now Cremilde was telling her that Julia had sent her a five-dollar bill which she had never changed, which she would show her along with some other things. As a child, Julia had had smallpox; she had tied up her hands; and day and night she had carefully daubed her face with sweet almond oil. She had come out of it unscathed, without a mark. The ache that gnawed at her was not having her all those years. She had fled to Spain, Julia had, and from there to America. The last letter she had written was from Venezuela, begging her mother's forgiveness for having abandoned her; saying that she was in search of a better fate. . . .

Returning to the room, Amelia noticed a number of objects piled on the chest of drawers. Cremilde, as if she had caught her glance: "I would like you to see it. Those are my treasures." She had seated herself on the edge of the bed and appeared terribly worn and tired out. And yet, with a strangely tranquil air, almost happy.

Amelia went to get the photographs. Cremilde explained, "Look at my husband, what a stout fellow! And Julia, isn't she smart?" Her godmother Rufina, may God be with her soul, had been like a mother to her. And the boy in the coffin, hands pressed together, a mop of hair, laced shoes. And again Julia, a little babe in arms, and again Julia, at her first communion. She then brought over the pocket missal, the moth-eaten fan, the small cane tray, and placed all of them next to the old woman who, with lowered eyelids, seemed to be meditating. They had finished their cup of tea, and Amelia was thinking about leaving.

"Are you feeling better?"

"Oh, much better," Cremilde hastened to reply. But please, she shouldn't go yet. Just a bit longer. She would like to lie down. She lifted her legs up with some effort, slid over on the mattress, covered herself with the bedspread, gazed at her benefactor: "I'm very old. . . . I'm seventy-nine years old." And wouldn't she like to amuse herself by reading the letters. They were from her husband to her during their courtship. Nicely written, a lovely script. João had gone to Business School. Just a bit longer. She was most grateful to her for having come. And, begging her pardon, she turned on to her right side, her face to the wall.

Amelia untied the stack of letters and began to read by the light of the kerosene lamp: "Lamego—Barracks of the 11th Cavalry—My Dear and Most Worshipped Cremilde—For me the greatest happiness is to see you. If only it could be every day! Later on, at Vespers, I'm going to bring the horses to drink at the Idol fountain and I'll pass your door. If your mother would permit you to come to the window . . ."

Allowing the letter to fall to her lap, Amelia began to mull over her meeting with Cremilde, the sudden illness of the old woman, the request she had made, the confidence she had shown in her. Were there then still such people? From now on how should I treat her? I can't, like before, give her some coins and continue on my way. She has shown herself to have a soul (perhaps it would be more exact to say: a character; yes, a character): she has her memories, her relics, a story to tell: happy and painful, and she so refined and filled with feelings. Well, this poor woman must be a special case. But who knows whether there might not be others like her? The poor. We meet them on a street corner, on the stairs of the subway, on a bench in the park,

MARIA ONDINA BRAGA

in tatters, old, lame. At home, however, what are they like? There in their shacks, their hovels? Might they not all have, like Cremilde, little subtleties, and family photos, and love letters?

Cremilde. The poor woman had brought a miracle into her life: that of believing in someone. She, Amelia, frightened of everyone and everything. A co-worker had asked her to go to the movies, to have a drink; she had wondered, "And what if he's married? What if he only wants to fool around with me?" She didn't go; she never went. And suddenly the desire to love and be loved came to her. Loneliness: an abyss open at her feet, a deep pool, a well. "My Dear and Most Worshipped Cremilde . . ." Julia beating her wings, like a migratory bird, headed for the land of adventure. Such birds sometimes fell from exhaustion in the middle of the ocean and drowned. Even worse if a creature drowns within itself.

She got up. She began to pace softly back and forth. And what if tonight it was she who spoke to Gustavo who had asked her out so often? What if she were to begin from now on to say yes? Not everybody was deceitful, after all. Cremilde hadn't deceived her; she really had needed her. For that alone, how grateful she was to her! She approached the bed and asked in a tender voice:

"Can you get on without me, now? Are you feeling better?"

The answer doesn't come. She insists: nothing. She bends over to watch the old woman sleeping. So calm one cannot even hear her breath. Her features in repose, her profile sharp: she looks like Julia—or like herself in her wedding picture. Amelia calls her softly by name. Silence. She looks around, not exactly afraid, but surprised. Where is she? How did she get here? Who? . . . She tries to control herself. Cremilde. She is in Cremilde's house, in the house of a friend. She cries out: Cremilde! She reaches forth and lightly places her hand on her forehead. That chill. A deeper chill. A chill that is not of this world.

Translated by Alexis Levitin

THE WORLD OVER THE OTHER FADED ONE

(excerpt)

by

Maria Isabel Barreno

MARIA ISABEL BARRENO

Maria Isabel Barreno, like her two collaborators in the New Portuguese Letters *project, was born in Lisbon (1939) and educated at the university there. Her interest in sociology took her to the Instituto Nacional de Investigação Industrial where, for thirteen years, she researched and wrote on labor issues. At the same time, Maria Isabel Barreno became one of Portugal's leading feminists. A co-founder of the Movimento da Libertação das Mulheres, she has been a major contributor to the literature of the women's movement. In the late 1960s, for example, she participated in a lecture series on the condition of Portuguese women, later published in book form by Urbano Tavares Rodrigues. A longer paper on the image of women in the press appeared in 1976.*

In the realm of fiction, in addition to New Portuguese Letters, *Barreno has authored novels and collections of short stories, most, though not all, dealing with women's issues. Of particular interest for feminism is* A Morte da Mãe *(The Death of the Mother, 1979) which successfully fuses her interests in sociology and fiction. It is a novel that exposes, in a highly imaginative vein, the process of women's subjugation throughout time: from the original biological cell and an initial matriarchal period to patriarchal domination and eventually to a contemporary historical moment that threatens to reverse the process and reestablish a matriarchal order.*

Barreno's short stories are less exclusively feminist in orientation; they focus instead on the dark and mysterious underside of a more generalized quotidian experience. The selection translated here is from the novella O Mundo Sobre o Outro Desbotado *(The World Over the Other Faded One, 1986). It is a work that explores the interstices between reality and fantasy: the relations between characters of flesh and blood and the relations between these "real" characters and visions or voices that eventually become flesh.*

Works by Maria Isabel Barreno

Adaptação do Trabalhador de Origem Rural ao Meio Industrial e Urbano, *1966*
Os Trabalhadores e o Progresso Técnico, *1967*
De Noite as Arvores São Negras, *1968*
Os Outros Legítimos Superiores, *1970*
Novas Cartas Portuguesas, *1972*
A Imagem da Mulher na Imprensa, *1976*
A Morte da Mãe, *1979*
Inventário de Ana, *1983*
A Dama Verde, *1983*
Contos Analógicos, *1983*
Sinos do Universo, *1984*
O Falso Neutro, *1985*
Célia e Celina, *1985*
O Mundo Sobre o Outro Desbotado, *1986*
O Enviado
Crónica do Tempo, *1991*
O Chão Salgado, *1992*

THE WORLD OVER THE OTHER FADED ONE

Margarida had given up her visits to the psychiatrist. It bored her, sitting in that consulting room with its functional furnishings, telling things which were interesting only when she experienced them.

"I'm wasting time and money for nothing," she thought.

The psychiatrist had strenuously insisted that Margarida not make such a decision.

"You're going to regret it. You can't leave your treatment before it's over. You'll start suffering the anguish you felt before."

The psychiatrist enumerated all the reasons except the one closest to the truth: that he would miss hearing the discourse that Margarida brought him, even though it was second-hand or in a second voice, even though it was reported and fragmented. That angered Margarida; she was normally susceptible to even the

---

From *O Mundo Sobre o Outro Desbotado* (*The World Over the Other Faded One*), by Maria Isabel Barreno (Lisbon: Rolim, 1986).

THE WORLD OVER THE OTHER FADED ONE

worst influences of others, but that made her decision to desist irrevocable.

Not many days had passed when the psychiatrist telephoned, asking her if he could stop by. Margarida didn't have the slightest interest in seeing him now.

She hadn't experienced any of her former anguish nor was she regretting her decision. Everything around her had changed.

Nowadays there were lots of people who had hallucinations, and quite a few spoke about them openly without any problem whatsoever.

Quite a few people, in certain environments and certain circles. In those cases, the ability to hallucinate was considered proof of imagination, or even of creativity—of course this was implicit and never expressed as theory.

Some, the types who always try to stand out from the crowd by saying things of absolutely no importance, declared:

"Hallucinations exist, and it is therefore necessary to keep the spirit open to receive them," and they smiled, as if to suggest that the "bourgeoisie" would never experience such ecstasies.

Clearly not, as evidenced by those very speakers. It was likely that still others brazenly lied, inventing marvelous sounds and images when in fact they remained in the most complete silence, in the most absolute darkness.

All of this allowed Margarida to rejoin in good stead the company of her friends. A few were a little upset when she stopped going to the psychiatrist, others continued expressing fears and concerns because that was their nature; but the vast majority asked her curious questions, and a few said they shared her fate as a hearer, or they claimed to be seers. Margarida had gained a new popularity, although that, at times, bored her.

But when the psychiatrist called, asking to drop by, Margarida acquiesced, giving in once again to her listless desire not to hurt anyone.

The psychiatrist came, had a whiskey, asked a few questions. That visit was followed up by various others, until Margarida sensed that he had managed to reinstate their former situation, the difference being that the "consultations" were now in her house, and that she didn't have to pay him, just give him whiskey. The psychiatrist continued listening avidly.

MARIA ISABEL BARRENO

When she realized this situation, Margarida had an angry reaction, like all those who find themselves drifting into realities imposed by others who are more aggressive:

"What a life," she thought, "going around as the spokesperson for the invaders while next to me is a man with whom I don't even have a friendly relationship."

As soon as she thought this, the phrase "spokesperson for the invaders" struck her as odd. Why had it occurred to her? Had she heard it before without consciously remembering it?

Margarida was thinking about the best way to get rid of the psychiatrist, when her boyfriend decided to come to her rescue.

The two were eating lunch, Margarida and the boyfriend, in a pastry shop after their respective days at work. She, a little removed, and using the boyfriend for the moment merely as a distant listener, was lamenting her fate:

"Why the devil do I have to put up with that man? I have to find a way to get free of him. I don't even like him."

The boyfriend immediately jumped into the monologue:

"What? He's visiting you? He doesn't leave you alone? But this is incredible! Tell him that it's me who doesn't want you seeing him."

Margarida half closed her eyes and had various reactions. She marveled at the fickleness of human beings: not too long ago the boyfriend, a stolid, true-believing economist, strongly advised her to continue her visits to the psychiatrist; now, with the visits becoming slightly less formal, he was strongly opposed to them. She knew he was trying to make a joke out of it, to be her accomplice, offering her that idiotic excuse, easily accepted especially by a psychiatrist; she knew too that he was only partly joking, that he was in fact jealous, much more than he would admit to himself.

She almost used that pretext: to excuse herself because of a man—wasn't that one of the advantages women always took from their situation, leaving men with all the indignities of power?

At the same time she reacted against the idea. She felt detached from the psychiatrist and even further removed from the boyfriend: what constantly absorbed her now were those ethereal fragments of a discourse.

She confined herself to responding:

THE WORLD OVER THE OTHER FADED ONE

"What nonsense!"
As one might expect, the boyfriend reacted in turn, and badly. He felt that to be a duty inherent in his role. He lost his playful tone and made a jealous scene. He took her refusal and her aloofness as signs of interest in the psychiatrist, and he got very angry. Had he the smallest bit of intelligence, he might have known that if she were thinking about the psychiatrist at all, it would be in a negative way. His anger grew, and as always happens, he found deep within himself all the justifications for his frenzied soliloquy.

"Go right on seeing him if you want," he concluded. And he left her right then and there in the pastry shop.

She waved at him absentmindedly while eating a cream tart. She saw him leave her field of vision, like a small object overwhelmed by the distance. She thought about the psychiatrist, avidly installed in her living room. In the foreground, right next to her ear, voices whispered. She asked herself,

"What do I expect from all of this in the end?"

Without an answer that might help her, she went back home.

On her way home, Margarida cut across a little garden in the center of the square near the road where she lived. She noticed, somewhat absentmindedly, a little old man staring at her. Her feet continued on their way while her head kept on with its ruminations. Without knowing why nor how, Margarida found herself sitting on the bench alongside the old fellow. He greeted her very delicately, lightly tipping his hat.

"Good afternoon. I feel I know you."

Margrida gave him a second look, this time with some attention.

"I don't know, I don't think I know you, but if you're in the habit of coming here, it's possible, since I live close by."

"Yes, but I don't think it was here that I saw you." The old man seemed certain.

Margarida didn't respond.

"I'll introduce myself: my name is Santos, José dos Santos," said the fellow, who seemed to like his name even though, or perhaps because, it wrapped him in perfect anonymity. "Don't you normally hear things, some sentences, voices?"

Margarida was taken aback:

"How do you know that?"

MARIA ISABEL BARRENO

"Look, I don't know how to explain it to you. It's just that as soon as I saw you I had this impression. You know, I see things, strange people passing by."

"You?! You have visions?!" Margarida was amazed. Closed off in her own world, she thought the rest of society was without imagination, creativity or eccentricity.

"That's right. Little old me."

Margarida looked at this specimen of the bowing and scraping petty bourgeoisie and didn't want to believe it.

Their conversation seemed promising, but just then a chubby and smiling woman, between forty and fifty years old, appeared.

"Allow me to introduce Odete, my very good friend. Odete isn't like us, but she understands everything very well, she always understands me. If only everyone were like her—the doctors, nurses, assistants, people like that—then all that commotion going on out there would never have started."

Dona Odete looked at senhor Santos with a smiling, benevolent affection. For some unknown reason, Margarida felt that the presence of the old man's friend had brought an end to the conversation. She got up and continued on her way.

The following day, in the evening, Margarida, still immersed in her strange aloofness—"like a spell," she thought—sat down in her living room in front of the desk.

This desk had a function difficult to put into words, but it was nonetheless important. Margarida used it to write letters, to jot down the events of the day and her feelings on small pieces of paper that never went anywhere, to do her accounts, and to think comfortably, with her elbows supported, as she doodled on a tablet of paper—the same tablet that she used to do her accounts, to write letters, and so forth.

The telephone rang. The psychiatrist was in a booth on the corner, and asked to come over just for a few minutes, a short visit. She sighed and said all right—it was only when she was required to actively participate in other people's lives that she was capable of strong and unexpected resistance.

He entered, discreetly, and collapsed on a pillow on the floor, sitting in a buddha position. Nowadays he regularly adopted this and other oriental postures, convinced that in doing so he was cleansing his organism from the evil influences of society. It cost

THE WORLD OVER THE OTHER FADED ONE

him a great deal, clearly visible in the way his joints were awkwardly contorted.

Margarida left him to his pillow and his lotus position and remained silent—she did this more frequently now. A subtle change had taken place within her. She no longer got angry with herself when she limply allowed others into her life. She no longer allowed herself to be concerned with those others, the invaders. She no longer dragged along those clinging personalities, the parasites of her existence.

But the psychiatrist didn't give up visiting her. He waited, having aggressively fostered within himself the patience of an oriental. He had long ago relinquished his guise of a conscientious, hard-working scientist.

She sat down again in front of the desk, doodling and jotting down absurd sentences. Stationed on his pillow, the psychiatrist, heroically, neither moved nor asked what she was writing.

The telephone rang again. It was the boyfriend. He too was close by and he also needed to see her right then. There was a great urgency in his voice:

"We have to have a serious talk. I think we should get married."

Bored, Margarida took this as a confirmation of how marriages were usually formed: as solutions for needs, irritations, and solitarily painful crises. Just a few days of absurd jealousy had transformed a detached boyfriend into a potential husband.

She avoided mentioning the psychiatrist, she just told him she wanted to be by herself. But he knew that an outright refusal would never come from her alone, and he inferred that the psychiatrist was there. He shouted till he got hoarse, and then hung up on her.

"Two days from now he'll be back talking about marriage with even greater urgency and conviction," sighed Margarida. She returned to her activities, going back and forth between them entirely at will.

Suddenly Margarida heard a tiny noise in a corner of the room. She looked: a tall figure of a woman dressed in an undefinable luminous color was coming, apparently, from that corner.

Her hands carried a luminous box, and she crossed the room magnificently. When she passed in front of Margarida, she

stopped, slowly turned her head, and looked Margarida in the eyes, saying,
"Pay attention, Margarida."
And in that brief instant, during which Margarida gave her all her attention, irresistibly drawn to the woman's eyes, the entire world took on a different quality. And the woman, that very woman, was no longer merely a majestic figure. In all of her design and color, in all the delicate material network of which she was made, were expressed her multiple attributes, like vibrating cilia that make and erase landscapes: a welcoming lap, a firmness of pure ivory, a profound wisdom—yes, much more profound than that of all the dreams—an inexhaustible fountain of every kind of giving. And these attributes and their derivatives were not dispersed, they were a single, whole, cohesive existence. That was what the presence of that woman said.
The figure then turned her head and continued her proud march with the radiant box.
On his buddha cushion, the psychiatrist trembled, cleared his throat, and squealed:
"I saw her, I saw her!" as if he were announcing his first orgasm to the world.
"What did you see?" Margarida asked.
"I saw a splendid woman dressed in blue."
"Once again, the subjectivity of color. What for me is indefinable, for him is blue."
"She walked by in silence, with her hands raised in front of her as if she were bringing us an invisible offering," remarked the psychiatrist, excited by all that precious symbolism. "You didn't see anything in her hands?" Margarida inquired.
"No, her hands were empty," the psychiatrist confirmed.
"Interesting," she thought, "he didn't hear what she said to me nor did he see the box. The box was also meant just for me." She sighed in relief; she wasn't about to fill him in on anything that he had missed. She felt that his exploitation of her had come to an end, that the psychiatrist would give up his vampirism—not voyeuristic but auditive. He too wanted to proclaim his independence.
"Goddess of science," was the phrase that kept coming to Margarida's mind in the hours and days that followed. The

woman's intense stare, revealing all her qualities, continued to occupy Margarida's thoughts. But the more that instant of communion receded in time, the more those attributes, without losing any of their lasting meaning, became like lenses, transparent, aqueous, magnifying the qualities of this world: the beauty of the sun and gardens became acute to the point of making a person cry, the greatest misfortunes were found to contain the very purest signs of progress; the fabric of all reality was complete, without excesses or absences. "This is the look of that woman on the needs of our world," Margarida knew, and thus the phrase "goddess of science" occurred to her.

"I wonder how many goddesses of science there have been?" she added, "all of them transmitting the same thing to us over and over." The complete wisdom had trickled away through unsuspecting cracks more swiftly than water.

The psychiatrist quickly said goodbye that night. He felt, in fact, that he had received his share, compensation for his persistence—so great did the miracle that he had observed seem to him.

He left quickly, so that he might still have time that evening to make various calls to friends and colleagues. Considering the current environment in the sophisticated urban world, he saw himself as a chosen one, gifted. The following day, he would continue with calls, letters, and phrases that, with supposed carelessness, he would let drop in conversations. He saw himself moving right along on the golden road to success.

In fact, he thought his compensation to be so satisfactory and definitive, that after that night he saw Margarida only a few more times. He no longer had any need of her, now that he was her equal.

Margarida also didn't think about him very much. Just as she acquiesced in seeing him, she was relieved not to have to put up with him any more, and didn't feel the bitterness one normally feels when discarded.

A few days later, always out of step, the candidate for bridegroom appeared.

"I want to marry you right away," he insisted.

Margarida looked at him, pensively.

"I think you can rest easy now," she informed him. "The psychiatrist is clearly going to stop visiting me."

"Why?" asked the uneasy fiance. He was a pessimisitic man.

"Because he finally got what he wanted," Margarida couldn't resist amusing herself a little, the naughty girl. People always ready to be crucified irritated her.

"What?" squealed the bridegroom candidate.

"He managed to share in one of my visions."

"What??!!" the candidate resquealed.

"He saw a woman, the same one I saw, crossing my living room," Margarida explained succinctly. She never confided the particularities of her visions to that boyfriend, and she was much less inclined to do so now.

"But now that you two have shared so much," continued the obtuse bridegroom candidate, "now he'll redouble his visits to you."

Margarida lost her patience.

"Stop with this foolish jealousy, and see if you can't act with some degree of intelligence."

And she left him, this time firm in her resolve to be more definitive. Premarital scenes between couples always gave her an acute acid stomach.

Translated by Darlene J. Sadlier

HOUSES IN THE SHADOW

(excerpt)

by

Maria Velho da Costa

MARIA VELHO DA COSTA

Maria Velho da Costa, one of Portugal's most distinguished novelists and one of the famous Three Marias, was born in Lisbon in 1938. Educated in a Catholic girls' school, she went on to take a degree in Germanic philology at the University of Lisbon. After holding various positions as a researcher and freelance teacher, she was appointed lecturer in Portuguese at King's College of the University of London, where she remained until 1987. At the time of this writing, she was Portugal's cultural attaché in Cape Verde. She has also been president of the Portuguese Writers' Association and, with the other Marias, an active member of the now-defunct Movimento da Libertação das Mulheres.

Maria Velho da Costa has published over a dozen books, among them the now classic Maina Mendes *(1969) and the prize-winning novels* Casas Pardas *(*Houses in the Shadow, *1977),* Lucialima *(1983), and* Missa in Albis *(1988). She is a difficult writer who molds language as others mold clay. Word play, syntactical fragmentation, multiple intertextual references, and polyphonic structures are the hallmarks of her art. Thematically, it is the contemporary Portuguese scene that absorbs her, the plight of women but also of men, the domestic realities of her characters but also the reality of modern Portuguese history, in short, the response to oppression and colonialism of various kinds.*

The selection translated here is from Casas Pardas, *a novel that examines the lives of three female figures: an aspiring young writer attempting to come to terms with and perhaps even redeem the world around her; an older sister trapped in a smothering middle-class marriage; a domestic servant struggling to make a go of* her *life and marriage. The author tells their stories in a polyphonically-structured work that sensitively explores the complexities of the women's experience at the same time that it experiments with the many dimensions of form and style. The translator has chosen a selection that simultaneously captures the essence of the young writer and alludes to the Portuguese/African encounter. He has retained syntactical fragmentation and ambiguity, the English, French, Spanish, and German that appear in the text and the author's footnotes. The puns unfortunately could not always be accommodated by the English language.*

Works by Maria Velho da Costa

O Lugar Comum, *1966*
Maina Mendes, *1969*
Ensino Primário e Ideologia, *1972*
Novas Cartas Portuguesas, *1972*
Desescrita, *1973*
Cravo, *1976*
Português, Trabalhador, Doente Mental, *1977*
Casas Pardas, *1977*
Da Rosa Fixa, *1978*
Corpo Verde, *1979*
Lucialima, *1983*
O Mapa Cor de Rosa, *1984*
Missa in Albis, *1988*
Dores, *1991*

HOUSES IN THE SHADOW

I am going to wash and go for a walk in the poplar groves at the Zoo on the other side of town. The way over will be peaceful—the sun at nine o'clock is all fluid and smooth. I'll be wearing,

something old
and something new
something borrowed
something blue:

A necklace from my grandmother Elisa, the Crazy One, who used to go dressed up in bustles to the prison for liberals at Estoi to visit her favorite enemy—first cousin and husband; a letter from the illegitimate son that Sarah chucked out of the house and who is doing studies on pulsation at Champigny; a copy of Mensagem that I helped myself to from the back shelves of the

---

From *Casas Pardas* (*Houses In the Shadow*), by Maria Velho da Costa (Lisbon: Moraes, 1977).

HOUSES IN THE SHADOW

library; a pair of jeans Made in the USA, denim is also blue, oh skies above, you make me blue. I'm not one who changes because of what I perceive, rather, things change perceiving me. Or not, brothers Vladimir and Vladimir. It's too bad I don't have any kind of political sense beyond the purely day-to-day and local goings on. I should sign up for a course somewhere. But March isn't a month for moves like that. So when I think I deserve a rest, I go to the Zoo, to review, matter and consciousness and how they go together. Listen now with full attention because the earth changed color. It's well into the night, crystal clear, one o'clock in the morning rather severe. I think I'm in a state of shock. The serpent paralyzed by the stare of the serpent ought to beget the serpent so that, in the tradition of the Ancients, the tale of the land of paradise can begin:

    The Zoo on a weekday morning, I see it like a starry space within intersecting planes of glass, prisms. Not a high space or low. It is blue, transparent, grayish-blue. Cool and quiet. Right away the entrance is very mysterious, with its stone-slab floor hollowed out by steps, the same ones the cathedral has around the tomb of the kings, tickets handed in at the window, and there's the murmuring, eyes always down. Then, a small cupola, still covered, under a passageway closed off by frigid wire. It opens up to the green area and to the trees with the sand pathway, old metal structures and small pavilions with bandstand-style roofs. A bridge covered with rust, with volutes and colonnades, is suspended over a black, lifeless lake where wooden sea gulls, like eucalyptuses, shed layers of old paint. Shadows of fish emerge from water thick with mud, creating the illusion of great depth. From the small tile bench set into the wall that goes around the lake one could hear squawking, a nest of gulls spills over its halo of twigs, and perching above, all black and white, the slender sentinel of the skies. The flamingos turn red, their feet pondering in the shallower water, the coarse grass stands erect, knife blades open. An old man passes by with two empty metal buckets, a benevolent church bell somewhere punctuates the white-blue stillness where the pungent peace of the city resides. One walks along the base of an empty restaurant, a heavy shadowed kitchen woman with cock's comb hair setting small wrought-iron tables, thin pieces of English cake, still lukewarm, on an old, generous tray with dark wax

MARIA VELHO DA COSTA

finish. The white cockatoos with yellow-white feathers blink lazily, occasionally puffing up their chests in greeting, moving forward with an excited waltz step, then settling down again in their spacious cages along which the ivy spirals and twists. On the left side, greenhouses with frosted glass, all closed up, roses in bloom, another old man clutches his galvanized watering can. The rosebushes blazoned with name plates for park and bed locations don't seem to perfume the surrounding air. Instead, the zoo's own smells prevail; the snorting of the bovines, damp feathers and hair, the ground, the dung. Up above, branches join over pathways, there's no wind, no rustling of leaves. Everything suspended. Following a hierarchy of strongest fliers and the most dangerous on down, the predatory birds are in a huge dome with bars, dull brown feathers with the cold-fire eyes of soaring eagles and vultures above their prey. Because of an ancient pact between us, I know that the adult hawks acknowledge me. Down below, the tiger owls sleep with their white-feathered antennae out. With a piece of old blackened meat held firmly beneath one claw on the cement floor covered with watery droppings, a huge crow caws, breaking its food apart, its head cocked to one side, dismissing me. In the bush areas are the climbing birds, in the nets to the side are the more restive ones, the love parakeets with their waxen beaks. But the big climbers, the macaws, sit and stare. Thick rings under their eyes, sumptuously colored, icons, opaque stained glass windows with bold lines, long silver-yellow tails suspended in the great silence, yearning for dense greenness and thick humidity where they would really dazzle. Beyond, a female bison has just given birth, the old man with his buckets, immensely fatigued at the entrance of the animal shrine, one of several with mosque-style open doorways, circular in shape, made out of brick and limestone, the other big mammals, the dark buffalo, the deer with follicular armor covered by silky wool, the haunches of the pregnant zebra mare with her uncanny stripes. The giraffes gracefully hold their muzzles high, with flesh-like horns, their necks and legs on a line with the rock fissures, velvet soft eyes, camels curl their lips gently under the rolls of their humps, the buffaloes sleep in dust like that on far-off treks across the plains, their great smooth horns, white, like commas, signs from some ancient liturgical text. The newborn calf, unsteady on its feet, comes close, its ungainly head next to the metal fence, the

HOUSES IN THE SHADOW

sticky surface of its body tightening up, the mother bleating musically, calling to it, a mass of blood-soaked ashen skin hanging down from her hindquarters, I speak to the small one that is trembling and accepting my scratching of its still wet head, Go on, Go on, and I move away, my fingers smelling salty sweet, a group of colts cut loose, startled by the baptism of afterbirth, and by my compassion. A female chimpanzee extends its hand, acting out the social code without conviction. Around her neck she has one of her young, wrinkled, bright and curious, its head twisted around to see, arms holding onto the mother tightly, her pink nipples like coral under her upper body hair. But the gorillas seem in their death throes inside their glass-enclosed pavilion, under the blue-black hair, their eyes sage, pupils turned up, inert limbs belonging to an animal profoundly calm, openly mortal. Off to the side, the venerable orangutang, the exact living replica of all primates, the long fulvous hair lifting seductively with the movement from bar to bar—behold the wonder on the branch, the splendrous simian which truly flies, in its own slow way, the light of its fur and the gold of its eyes, its hair flowing from all over its body, fragile and sterile in captivity. The smell of the beasts is close now, rotten meat and feces fermenting. All of this is going on in a big open space, where the small monkeys constantly negotiate with everything around them, screaming and chattering angrily, then all of a sudden becoming gentle, like small siblings precariously inhabiting the same space, whatever they have; it's not from being so intelligent that they die in small and unfamiliar spaces, but rather the strict sense of loyalty to space that they develop. What species are we? The lions sleep. Twin cubs with round noses and ears, on top of their mother's huge soft paws, fight over a bone with red grooves. The large eyes are innocent, like a dog's, kind, like the mother's. The tigers already avoid eye contact, they never traffick in pleasure, recognition, in having offspring—they pace back and forth, slow and graceful, not like the bears who stretch out their lower necks, hitting the water in search of peanuts, a crust of bread, thrown there, I remember. Now the bears are sleeping on their backs, under the white sun, their coats stained by the dirty water, yellowed with age, the fetid smell of fish remains, ammonia odor coming from the pit. Without looking at me, the

MARIA VELHO DA COSTA

tiger keeps track of the distance between us from eyes behind black and gold stripes, deliberately ignoring me, so determined to insult even though I say, Greetings, master of solitude, in a loud voice, indistinct, Your fearful symmetry, invoking Blake. A pair of black panthers retreat to the darkest corner of their cell, four points of light ready to burst out at any moment. On the crushed stone pathway, my feet rub inside my high boots, forming blisters. Here you have the story of the colonizer's daughter, out of breath and limping, carrying the *Times*. I won't go see the wolves with the jerky motion they make when they reach the end of their run, tails down, solar eyes. Do they have yellow eyes because they are the wildest or the most solitary or is it mostly because they are predators who hunt at dusk and stare at the setting sun? I'm not going to see the wolves, they are my compatriots, they come from areas where the air is rarefied, from the mountains, the steppe, from the brushland, they are Europe, my part of Europe, even more than the bull, they are the howl in the cathedral, the paw extended to the demented monk, the student of cliffstone lancers and druids,[1] the secret alibi in the mistletoe and serpent of the desires of young maidens and old women in red hoods,[2] the collective devourer, the crafty loner, the animal that defines the boundary line of Europe up there by the Ural Mountains with its seemingly dog-like stature, its nature and wildness, Brother Wolf, the hirsute one.[3] I didn't see the wolves today, their blue and sticky desolation like the young woman's, that lethal fragileness of helpless maidens the city of Lisbon keeps locked up in its zoo, this testimony to an inability to behave imperially without thirsting for early death, without the swoonings of a fragile virgin, this tragic and transfigured relationship that the city maintains in its display of wild beasts taken by force from other lands. In its animal park, Lisbon is like a delicate child that at the age of eight dies with a strong sense of the futility of its own destiny, covered with lilies, having drifted off placidly from an illness with no suffering or agitation. But to see this, it has to be in the morning during the week, when the sun is tentative, when the roller skating rink is

---

[1] Reference to the novel by Aquilino Ribeiro, *Quando os Lobos Uivam* (*When the Wolves Howl*).
[2] Obvious reference.
[3] A less obvious reference.

HOUSES IN THE SHADOW

deserted and the children's park, with its just-so miniature houses and little cups and saucers, is empty, and the guinea pigs and the pink-eyed white rabbits run about in fetidness hard to describe, without any chorus of voices at the emergence of their hapless victim noses from ridiculous looking houses, and when there's no one on the see-saws with the colored seat backs and the cross-bars down. Because, with children and bright sunlight everything changes. It's best to go there when the animals don't act as if they were brought there and kept under great duress, when the setting is reminiscent of the 1900s, statues full of cracks and turrets that have turned greenish-gray. It's really pleasant then under light that seems unchanging, simultaneously violent and veiled, and my country so desperate in its invocation of twin souls in everything, desperate in its inability to maintain distance on itself which is the greatest qualifying ingredient for anyone wanting to tame someone else, Ah, go see the almost natural conditions in which the pandas peel the asparagus stalks in Regents Park, where the nocturnal animals, with the discreet use of light, have had their sleeping-waking cycle reversed—you will see the expansionist capacity of a nation untouched, the genesis and possibility of transplanting a colonial vocation, self-satisfied stupidity, complaisance, and artful deceit. What I'm saying is that the Lisbon Zoo has the perfect charm of a sad and dejected Alice, determined to die smiling, but without her cat, a very precise resolve. A special kind of Portuguese Preciseness.

The name Elisa, what does that mean—the Chosen one, the select-ed, the elected, rejected, the eliminated? Elisions avoid omissions. Is it that elections prevent the full-scale use of force, is it the avoidance of the argument for force? The delectable one. One who delectates, for what end? I was thinking about my name when I reached the elephant in these Elysian fields, sanctimonious, posthumous, this Zoo right here. But the elephant, largest of the proboscideans and the largest of the quadrupeds, has a twenty-two month gestation cycle. The elephant, the Chosen presence, the majestic animal, capable of vanishing at the slightest sound, unique for its hide and tusks, dense, white, sculptured, the base of rare inscriptions, always at the center of the spoils of war and of projects for patience and peace, its trunk its trumpet; according to legend, leaving communal death signatures on the surface of the earth. The majestic one that

MARIA VELHO DA COSTA

never sheds blood, El, Al, o Que. Eloi, Eloi. Subject only to fire, to droughts, to man—extreme needs. Don't be afraid, Elisa, they gestate for a long time.

ENUNCIATION

On the ground, beyond the trench, there were clumps of hay strewn around and heaps of thick, coarse dung, dark. It's a big area. From the parapet of the trench containing greenish water coagulated with coins, on a steep bank bristling with the edges of crushed stone, one can see the inside of the shelter, the darkness, the barrenness, and the immense, ash-colored form upside down. This is it—the ears are the wide ones of the great African, small and slow-moving eyes topped by thick hair, identical to the almost pathetic tuft at the end of the short, tapered tail. Huge toenails, a front leg raised, growing pinkish towards the knee area with the rose-colored light, and in the effort to stretch and move the great mass of wrinkled skin and deeply-set muscles towards the front, the great toenails, almost black, dig in but barely protrude beyond the abruptly ending foot, like a bulging tree cut off below the wide-joint. The two huge tusks serrated at the base, with striations of a chestnut tree, the thin lips raised, the small mouth almost coralline, hesitant. From it, the trunk reaches out full length, its wrinkles forming rings, with its dramatic cleft at the end, finely tuned, made for suction and seizing branches, quivering and probing, the membrane exposed, moist, timidly taking hold of the hand that strokes it, the beautiful, large hand with the glistening blackness of a sea animal surging from the water, bluish from the cold, the knots of powerful fingers showing clearly with the caressing movement, the palm closing gently, almost white, as if anointed with ashes, blue-black rose with its corolla hidden from the quivering soundings of the trunk of the great animal soothed by the voice affectionately making guttural sounds and clicks of the tongue, by the short, light, deep-set nails that gently and rhythmically massage the edge of that living, restless cleft. It was then that I heard him say to me very distinctly, Don't be afraid, Elisa. Leaning against the parapet a few feet away, watching all this, I

HOUSES IN THE SHADOW

said then, What? and he responded slowly turning towards me his onyx eyes with their resplendent acid-white, almost blue, background, maintaining his compassionate smile, I didn't say anything ma'am. Adding to the brusqueness of my gesture and to my fear of God's creatures was the pachyderm righting itself on all fours, withdrawing and raising up its sumptuous instrument like a bell, its cracked metal ringing out three times—At times we say things, we speak, without talking. My name is Elisa. In the presence of such an obvious display of sovereignty, it came out just like that. He was extremely tall, lean without being too thin, his full shoulders drawn back, round and compact under the gabardine coat which was almost white, his pants nonchalantly matching, a knife-edge pleat extending down to an exquisite foot, something out of Cardin or even Rome, the silk cuffs and front of his shirt, the same blend of white, muted browns, and black in the tie, the same narrow shoes, with not too much of a shine. The almost translucent nostrils of the short, firm-lined nose, arched slightly, forming an angle with the contours of his smile, pronounced cheekbones rising from his face, two raised areas spanned the expansive forehead just below a dense, curly head of black hair, the back of his neck shown perfectly smooth light nocturnal water. The light shed steel on the wide jaw, fell to the graceful carriage of the neck, the ash-blue wrist of a hand raised in the air to the sky, to me, was circled by a knotty cord of a heavy scar, the row of perfect teeth almost translucent, the full mouth slightly ironic, destroying my gesture with a look that seemed to barely tolerate the stupid ritual of a meek young girl, Pleased to meet you also, my name is Angelo. But something changed in shaking hands with him, there was an acknowledgment that it was good. Then he said, Don't be afraid, Elisa. And I mumbled under my breath, Hare Krishna. And he said, as if he were talking about the weather, Things on the continent aren't so good. He went on after sensing that I was staring at him, You're pale as a ghost, don't you want to sit down? And then, Are you Portuguese, are you sick? I'm Portuguese, yes, and I guess I could be sick, yes. And using informal address, Where are you from? He was shy, that was it, or he was an African leader from one of the embassies, or something even higher, royalty. Cape Town, he said with a malignant smile, but it wasn't directed at me, lame bird left

MARIA VELHO DA COSTA

behind. La illah ila Allah,[4] he said further, pensively, the label outside the sheer silk socks, the delicate ankle. Ai u é, I added. If you know any news of my Friend, he laughed along with me, and for the first time he touched me on the forehead with the three middle fingers of his right hand, saying, Malinke, *mia senhor fremosa,* somewhere in the backwaters of the great river, it really doesn't matter much. An island? I said. No, a forest will do, the humid heat will make the navels of the gods iridescent.

—You speak Portuguese well, I said, using the intimate form.

—When the Pentecost is born it is for everyone. It's the language of the soul.

—And your mother?

—When my mother was pregnant she went out to the edge of the river in search of the spirits of the ancients. There there was a crocodile, still young, that said to her, Kill me. My mother grabbed a big stone to crush it. The stone turned into a huge white owl that said to her, Place me on top of the crocodile and lay down on your belly in the sand until you stop hearing the sound of the stream. My mother did just that and when everything was very still, she opened her eyes in time to see a black panther heading towards the water, then raising a paw and staring at her with eternally angry eyes, saying, When you reach the village, slaughter a kid goat and cry out until all the great men and women are gathered there. You're going to give birth today but you will not feel any pain. When the child is born, anoint it with fresh blood of a dog and with the yellow of a chicken egg. You will say that you were already told this by the ancients who, accordingly, closed your body in anticipation of great deeds. See to it that your child grows up with a fear of buffaloes and of men with long hair. Such is the wish of the ancients. And having said this, the panther returned to its den in the river waters which once again had begun to murmur. And so it was.

—A kind of jungle version of Siegfried, *are you kidding?*

—*Quite so,* little Brunhilde, all European Amazons love exotic myths.

—But I am a *bajuda*[5] from Dahomey.

---

[4]God is the only God. Portuguese West Africa.
[5]Word for young girl in the creole of Portuguese West Africa.

HOUSES IN THE SHADOW

—You know a lot, my pretty gazelle, where are you running off to?
—*Ce n'st pas juste, je ne t'ai posé que des questions évidentes.*
—*L'évidence est une qualité de surface.*[6]
—*Ah, Ambiguous Adventure,* are you an animist or have you been Islamized?
—For one who has read so much, my gazelle, this is a stupid question. Isn't it important to you to know about those who touch you in some way?
—You weren't really touching me, you already did that, but you were impressing me with all the things you know.
—You're right, at times I'm apt to act like a Greco-Roman black man, here, that is. It's the slave legacy.
—Where, here?
—Europe.
—Were you educated here?
—I'm still being educated, only, there.
—I'm trying to dis-educate myself.
—That's very European, were you around for May of 1968?
—No, I'm going to be on earth in the year two thousand, with a big, big, tropical pine tree growing out of my hair.
At that point, he became silent, weighing the air around us and said:
—I'm sorry but you're the first Portuguese woman I suspect will be.
—Is there a lot of hate between us, prince?
—Well, to us it seems that way.
—Are you hiding something?—what are you doing here, what did you want from the elephant?
—I'm doing a service, I'm trying to serve, I became a bridge, I think.
—Africans prefer to speak through metaphors, as I do,
—Primitive peoples, whoever returns, the . . .
—Say it, say it,
—Black brothers.
—You don't seem black to me.
—To my people I am, to whites I am.
—Your people?

---
[6]Reference to *L'Aventure Ambigue*, a novel by Sheik Hamidou Kane. Senegal.

MARIA VELHO DA COSTA

—I was born there.
—There?
—There, under the earth where the dead never rest, where there never is any clear line between a ray of lightning and the rage of God, where the spirit flows from the infection of the thorn, where humiliation made an enigmatic cyst out of truth and lies, because you and your people lost the earth, they lost the earth, they lost the earth for us,
—I don't have people.
—You're dying, my gazelle, you are dying like the ancients dissolving in liquid feces, bound for the Antilles, cast down on the torture press, feet garrotted, a suckling child, you are dying like those who return to my land to undo the magic in one day, to amputate the chestnut trees in one month, to violate the forest and the paths of the ancients, in two days.
—Is it necessary to know about the primitive, Angelo?
—Yes, it is necessary to know them, white-flower. Do you want to see the reptiles with me?
—I'd like to but I don't know if what I'm wearing . . .
—Poor little Cinderella without a thing to wear to the ball.
And then Angelo kissed me on one of my eyes with great tenderness and, giving me even more delight, with longing and nostalgia. His mouth had the smell of incense, like mint crushed in a walnut pestle. The pleasure was pungent. I saw him speak to the snakes. A huge python began to slide along the trunk towards the glass of the enclosure, towards the voice, towards the eyes that were turning yellow and losing their pupils, narrowing to slits in fixed concentration, the arm raised in an almost imperceptible serpentine motion and the bifurcated tongue of the animal being invoked flicked in our direction, the neck twisted so that the small, taut, triangular head rested directly on the glass, I witnessed the pain. And he said,
—If it were in the forest and there weren't this plate of glass between it and us, would you be afraid?
—No, I said, with you I wouldn't be afraid of anything except separation.
—That's the only law, my gazelle.
I drank tea, he drank water, the two of us sitting under the trees, the cockatoos were asleep, the sun discernible, high overhead, filtered through high branches, casting rays over a carapace of

HOUSES IN THE SHADOW

clouds. The gypsy woman advanced towards us like a Nazarene boat, the hull absolutely silent and an immense eye at the stern, her skirts in waves, the netting of her sandals caressing the sand, a morning forewarning, the long guitar fingers, same stature as Angelo, haughty loins, moonscape face with small-pox craters, Would you like me to read your fortune, my young friend? You will travel great distances by sea in the company of a dark young man, you will hear the roaring of the depths and the creaking of the lines and hull. You will know hunger and thirst and your hair and fingernails will fall out but it will all be towards a good end. You will scare away monsters and heathens because you are good at heart and God-fearing. They will be putting you to the test of courage and you will have to walk over a bed of coals. You will have a boy child and girl child that will not repudiate their upbringing and one will depart for the north and the other for the south. There is someone who may wish you harm and who may want to involve your son in intrigue, a woman with blond hair who is dedicating nine days of prayer to your bad fortune, but you will not be unworthy of a lucky star and with the blessing of the master you will transcend the atmosphere to die in peace and with the esteem of all your people. That will be twenty escudos.
Angelo said:
—Where do you come from, mother of whiteness and color?[7]
—From the asshole of the ages, my dear black friend, from the asshole of the ages, where only God's clock is allowed.
—You said it, my dear sister, he responded.
And he gave her a bill for a hundred which made her smile slyly, for certain, she was a snake, or perhaps she looked that way because of the torn strips of cloth running like pieces of dry skin down her skirt to her feet, she proudly walked away like a bullfighter having just buried the sword, putting an end to a dangerous fight.
—They never do anything so they never stand to lose, all they do is transform by means of their perfect memories, I said.
—They never go back and they never advance, they merely change one thing for another, and die slow, proud deaths, but

---

[7]Paraphrase of the Conde de Vimioso, *Cancioneiro de Resende*.

MARIA VELHO DA COSTA

Frederico loved them.
—Who?, I said.
—Green green who loved us green.[8]
—Poets?
—Champions of hope for all of us, my gazelle, united and together.

More piercing than the sword was the experience at his house reminiscing about the tango. I say his house because he said,
—Do you want to come with me?
—Yes.
And I used the word yes which in Portuguese is seldom used by itself in an affirmative response.

The house wasn't very far, in the section called Blue, with its verandas and fat pretentious columns, the venetian blinds drawn, little creameries under stairwells, a place where there used to be tangerines growing, or am I just imagining something that never was. On the top floor to the right, Angelo put the key in the door leading to a small hallway with high door arches, frosted glass dividers leading to other rooms. I fixed my gaze on the arabesque designs of the Persian carpets that were laid out over one another covering all the floor area and on the luxurious plants in great white pots everywhere. There was no furniture, I don't think, just mirrors from different eras covering the walls above and below the paneling, at least in the room where I was that led to the veranda. Not one picture or oil painting. I expected to see masks, ivories, coats of arms, adornments, but all there was was mirrors, round ones, elliptical ones, slightly convex ones or huge flat glass surfaces with heavy precious metal frames, scrolls, other frames out of cashew wood, mahogany, thick bevelling without any matting, mirrors and more mirrors. They were terrifying walls with our reflections ad infinitum, walls to avoid. And there was the spacious veranda opening on the bleak backquarters, dozens of empty service staircases with their dented metal ramps going off at different angles, leading to vacant cement patios with lines and wires where fine apparel and other articles were hanging, still damp. Angelo's line was empty.

---

[8]Reference to F. Garcia Lorca.

HOUSES IN THE SHADOW

The Persian rugs undulated with their cornucopias and geometric petals in red and black, their somber greens, the top and bottom a dull turquoise color, the edges fraying. I took off my shoes. My blister glistened under the web of gauze, a bellflower, fragile and decaying. He had said, Wait here, and I overheard him engaging in titillations over the phone. Large climbing plants with wide, spatulated, star-shaped leaves nearly blocked the glass windows of the veranda, the hanging linen table cloth, worn, covered with large faded spots, filtered the light. It was beginning to rain again. I reclined against some sort of cushion with covers, the only piece of furniture there. When he returned, he said, This gadget, a big gramophone he got going without a crank. The sound was full, sharp, with just a little of the nasal quality immediately apparent in a rescued relic. It was then that I closed my eyes and saw them dancing to the same kind of wind-up phonograph, at the end of an afternoon with gold and chestnut hues, in the North somewhere, rough caned chairs in another ample veranda with a tile floor—the tango dancers, in perfect form, exquisite, she with a long-sleeved pearl crepe dress with button clasps and padding in the shoulders, he in a close-fitting suit and his hair, a shining metal plate fitted to the beautiful lines of his cranium, a deep furrow in the back of his neck, the two of them dancing without looking at each other, she with quick, stylized head movements, her neck tendons standing out like a noble diva's, he bracing her as she arches back from the waist over his hip, his hand fixed, white, almost blue, like a Greek statue, on her pliant waist which moves with the spirit of the dance, and he controlling the contest like a horseman's deft use of blinders and the bridle,

madreselvas en flor
que me vieran nacer
y en la vieja pared
sorprenderan mi amor
pasados los años
y los desengaños
el primer cariño
que nunca olvidé,

how old was I, two or three? it smelled like trays of fresh marmalade, coke iron, the presence was so strong. I opened my eyes

and said to Angelo.
—I think they were in love.
—It's not possible, it couldn't have been, here,

vieja pared
del arrabal
tu sombra fue
mi compañera
y todos los años
tus flores renacen
porque ya no muere
mi primer amor.

The trouble beat chords of the accordion, the drone of the raspy voice, the images of youthful Latin arrogance, of repressed passion and gallantry of fighting, like huge predatory birds, when I was a child, I probably watched them from the floor, in a state of ecstacy, feeling very small. Angelo, squatting on the other side, was wearing a somber, flowing tunic over his pants and bare feet, lightweight with open sleeves, the neck low-cut, and he looked at me, or beyond me, to them and said,
—Horse and beetle people of lapis lazuli, oarsmen of trireme that went up to the source of the Nile and descended to the mouth of the Niger?—no, they never could be in love without tearing each other to pieces.
—That's what happened.
Said I. And only then did I Understand. I hesitated and went on to say, You, who are you? and against the background of the burdened voice of Carlos Gardel, laden with the ages and transmigrations of spirit,

Asi aprendi que hay que
fingir
para vivir
decentemente,

Angelo began to move the erect trunk of his body in a swaying motion, singing in a very serious voice, accompanying himself with slow clapping, the thump of his knees on the floor muffled like cardiac percussion under the skin, a muted drum,

HOUSES IN THE SHADOW

ouvre à l'ombre de l'Homme
ouvre, ouvre à mon double
mon double viendra dire
tout ce qu'il aura vu
aux portes de l'empire
d'où les morts sont venus
ouvre à l'ombre de l'Homme
ouvre, ouvre à mon double.[9]

Then, for the first time I was afraid and he saw it. And kneeling at my side, with a cup full of hazelnuts in his hands, he said with great reverence, Fear Nothing, Elisa.

A woman with a very rich voice, very piercing, sang the praise La illah ila Allah, from the Koran, Where, where is this from? Guinea, my gazelle, the great remains of Mali, we also descend from the same stock, tribe against tribe, but the ancients keep vigil in the fibres of the aloe plant, under the skins of reptiles on the edges of great rivers. The woman's voice grew loud and harsh and I humbly took hold of the edge of his fine linen cambric, bringing it to the lips of my bowed head, to my cold forehead, to the space between my eyes. I saw then that his wrists were marked by deep lacerations all around as well as his bare ankles with their fine tendons and protruding bones. Still prostrate before him, I asked, Who wounded you? and he in turn told me, touching my chin with the tips of his fingers, his eyes on the fingers, he was someone who seemed to be suffering, *Sublimes excoriations d'une chair fraternelle et jusqu'aux feux rebelles de mille villages fouettés, arénes.*[10] Afterwards, he asked me,
—And you, what do you want, my young friend?
And I spoke, sounding like a naive queen at the beginning of her career:

Ah, if I could restore something for my people, it wouldn't be their pride, certainly not their pride, but the pleasure of being Being what?

---

[9]Birago Diop. Incantation. Senegal.
[10]Aimé Césaire. *Patience des Signes.* The Antilles.

MARIA VELHO DA COSTA

Being everything, humble, temperately, discreetly everything, peaceful, Portuguese
Wise in the ways of the world?
Wise in knowing, the way that animals know the world around them, like you people
We, the black people?
Yes, you, the people who are rising up from humiliation without identifying with those who have humiliated you
You're inventing all this, my gazelle, the flesh is ancient but the spirit is new on earth, it wasn't you that taught us violence, cannibalism exists in the memory of all mankind, in order for you to be able to talk with me, look at my clothes, there are thousands of other Africans sweeping your streets, but you don't discourse with them on matters of life and death. And loving care, passionate tenderness, passion diluting into the other, into the world
The patience of mothers with their offspring, is that what you want from your country, and from the people of Africa?
That's right, that's it
But you are full of hatred, terror, autos da fé, severe monuments, my gazelle
Like you, my sweet black panther, like you, the spire of Notre Dame is like your lost spear
Young maiden gazelle, respect the wrath of the poor. The ancient sword that sleeps in the forest under the chest of the hunted man isn't the bridge over the Tagus, it's more expensive, newer. There are no more chosen peoples, there are munificent survivals, it's something very different

But that's what I'm saying
You can talk about these things with me but at the same time you can't talk with me about them, the Africans aren't wadding for your wounds on earth, for your people
We are wounded people too, there are Portuguese sleeping under bridges, far away.
But they're not your people, from your flesh
Yes they are
Look at my wrists
Your scars are vainglory
My glory is coming here, naked in spirit, responding to what you

HOUSES IN THE SHADOW

say, coming across you and not being able to take you with me
Then nothing is possible?
I can put it off, my gazelle, our fatherlands cannot, our countries that begin at the end, I can't postpone that, however sweet that might be, *bai é magoado, mas se cabado, ca ta birado*[11]
Is that from Cape Verde?
It is, or putting it another way,
Every leaving is an alphabet that is born
every return a nation learning to spell
Every leaving Is power in death
And every return is childhood learning to spell[12]
Angelo, what I am looking for in this country and in everything else is a kind of lost magnificence or the chance to reinvent it, in its totality, like the black people whose dignity on this earth is total, like you
Dignified and vulnerable like species who tenaciously cling to their habitat
Like the mutants
Like love which is difficult after the death of noble sentiments, after the death of arbitrary unities between tribes and castes
Harmony on earth, with the earth, I want total harmony, Angelo
It's the desire of castes and peoples exhausted from suffering, from humiliation, you can go back to yourself, my gazelle, there are no more barriers for you
Do you believe that there's no salvation without violence?
Without organized vehemence, for the survivors, for the mutants, for the poor peoples of the world
What is the difference between violence and vehemence?
Vehemence can laugh at itself, it cries, grows tender with time, has setbacks, and goes on like a great love affair
That's weakness
That's a sign of strength.

In his right hand he had an old ivory band, polished, a deep, blackened crack cut through it from one side to the other, but somehow it held together, the edges worn by time and use.

---

[11]"Coming is gladness, parting is sadness, but one who never leaves cannot come back." Creole proverb. Cape Verde.
[12]Corsino Fortes. *Pão e Fonema.* Cape Verde.

MARIA VELHO DA COSTA

He put it on my right arm and I said,
—Are you leaving?
—I'm going to take you home
—Do you know Amilcar?
—Never ask about the whereabouts of heroes in the country of carp.
—Of the Parcae?
—No, of those carnivorous and long-living fish that reside in stinking pools impenetrable to memory. May I touch your head?
And his hands held my entire cranium, reaching down to the skin under the cold hair, along the ridge of skin of the two scars on the curve of the cheek bones, his warm fingers tracing the bristly roots of this gray scalp of mine, over the soft scrolls of what lay inside there was a corolla of flesh enclosing the cranium box and never more would there be bliss, never more the conjunction of separate things. It was nightfall, time for wolves, hour *di bai*.[13]

It's one o'clock in the morning. I am a European. My sister telephoned me, desperately needing help. It was nine then. Minutes later I asked the operators to connect me with another section of town, Azul, I will see you, my gazelle. Sleep in caves, you'll sleep well there. I asked for the address:
—I'm sorry, miss, this address doesn't have a telephone.
—Must be a mistake, I'm sorry.
It was time to get a cab, to go on up to what I already knew, to the famuli of the neighbor down below, a European:
—Look, my friend, this place has been empty for years now, nobody lives there, seems like the landlady is keeping it for some family members.
—From Africa?
My word, no, miss, from Linhó, a girl that is about to be married, the house is empty of furniture, from time to time the landlady's cleaning lady comes by to vacuum, get rid of the cobwebs.
—It doesn't have any carpets?
—Not a thing, miss, excuse me, miss, I'm sorry, it's clear that you're a fine young lady, are you interested in the house?—I

---
[13]Leaving. Creole. Cape Verde.

HOUSES IN THE SHADOW

mean, people like to know who's going to be above them.
It was Lala.
—No, that is, maybe, you didn't hear any noise this afternoon? At that point she turned cold, made an effort to close the door.
—No, miss, it must be a mistake, you'll excuse me but I have to go about my life.

But, at one o'clock in the morning on a clear night, I'm not bothered about the possibility of being crazy. I'll never tell the truth about what seems improbable. In these parts of the world, one has to get used to the improbable and its secret workings until some invisible stimulant brings reality to light. I switch my bracelet to the left wrist, the hand that endorses the space, uncertain where to sign. I hear, Bach, May I touch your head?

Bist du bei mir
geh ich mit Freuden
zum sterben und zu meiner ruh
Ach, wie vergnügt
wär so mein Ende,
es drückten deine schönen Hände
mir die getreuen Augen zu.[14]

I will sleep perhaps threatened by spotted Bambis, by silly looking wing-eared elephants flying around the forest, this forest with its cartoon design, May God save you from the proliferation of Disneyland, Angelus and may the earth shake, may it shake, this earth contaminated by incongruous inscriptions that I superimpose on it. This earth relentlessly transgressed gives signs, splits apart when it reaches the high register on our scale.

Is it necessary to change nature? I also said to him, still in his arms.
Which, our nature?
The nature of the earth.
Our nature is the nature of the earth.

Translated by Charles Cutler

---

[14]If you were to go with me, I would journey to my death and joyfully rest. Ah, how sweet my end would be if you were to close my faithful eyes with your hands, so beautiful. Stolzel. From the *Notebook for Ana Magdalena Bach* (1725).

EMMA

(excerpt)

by

Maria Teresa Horta

MARIA TERESA HORTA

One of the famous "Three Marias," Maria Teresa Horta was born in Lisbon in 1937. She first drew the attention of the literary establishment as a poet, a member of the group known as "Poesia 61." Espelho Inicial *(First Mirror, 1960) was the beginning of a poetic activity that has lasted more than two decades and has resulted in over a dozen additional volumes, including the controversial* Os Anjos *(The Angels, 1983) in which angels, far from being the disembodied spirits of religious fame, are decidedly erotic. Maria Teresa Horta's career as a novelist began a decade later with the publication of* Ambas as Mãos Sobre o Corpo *(Both Hands on the Body, 1970) and her fiction has continued to develop in tandem with the poetry. She had five novels published as of 1985. Horta is also a journalist. Throughout the 1970s, she edited the literary section of various well-known newspapers and she was for a long time the editor and literary and film critic of the magazine* Mulheres *(Women). Her interest in film also led to work with the ABC Cine Club in the 1960s and to the making of a film with António Macedo based on one of her poems.*

Novas Cartas Portuguesas *(New Portuguese Letters, 1972), which she published with Maria Isabel Barreno and Maria Velho da Costa, brought Maria Teresa Horta international fame as one of Portugal's leading feminists. Shortly after the Revolution of 1974, she became one of the co-founders of the Movimento da Libertação das Mulheres. That organization is now defunct but Horta found a place for her advocacy in the pages of* Mulheres.

It could be argued that Horta's literary work is of a piece. Verse or prose, her writing has a lyrical cast and abounds with the symbols and themes that serve as its common denominators. Mirrors are pervasive, for example, as is the concern for women's sexuality and for the need to free women's space from the bonds that have so long restricted it.

The selection translated here is taken from the novel Emma *(1985), which focuses on a theme common to Horta's two earlier* novels: the mental disintegration of a woman caught up in the sterility of upper-middle-class life, a world governed by convention and by male dominance. As in the earlier books, the protagonist's self-revelation (this time to a psychoanalyst) is in itself a liberating act, an attempt to exorcise a past that has led her to the brink of destruction. Formally, the passage illustrates Horta's play with narrative space, her tendency to arrange her prose on the page—at times only a few lines to a page—as a poet arranges her verse. The translator has used lines to indicate the author's spatial separations.

Works by Maria Teresa Horta

Poetry

Espelho Inicial, *1960*
Tatuagem *(Poesia 61), 1961*
Cidades Submersas, *1961*
Verão Coincidente, *1962*
Amor Habitado, *1963*
Candelabro, *1964*
Jardim de Inverno, *1966*
Cronista Não E Recado, *1967*
Minha Senhora de Mim, *1971*
Educação Sentimental, *1975*
Mulheres de Abril, *1977*
Poesia Completa, 2 vols., *1983*
Os Anjos, *1983*
Minha Mãe Meu Amor, *1986*
Rosa Sangrenta, *1987*

Fiction

Ambas as Mãos Sobre o Corpo, *1970*
Novas Cartas Portuguesas, *1972*
Ana, *1975*
Emma, *1985*
Cristina, *1985*

EMMA

She stares ahead, sitting in the rocking chair: straw and matte finish, smooth wood that she strokes softly with her fingers; scratching it lightly with her nails, barely touching, prudent, lest a trace be left.
"Prudently. Lest any trace remain of your passage through here. Any vestige."
"Emma."

(I don't understand, you know? Rather, I don't want to. All I remember is my hands covered with blood. All that blood, all that silence. That huge relief when I sat on the floor beside him, fallen onto the rug, the knife I carefully pulled out of his neck, leaving the wound open. My love, I said, my love, very softly: and this vertigo, this fright, this fear, this darkness, this recoil from myself. I killed you, I told him, avenged.

From *Ema* (*Emma*), 2nd ed., by Maria Teresa Horta (Lisbon: Rolim, 1985).

There were two of us, didn't you know? Two every day, two step by step between willing and obeying, between love and hatred. My love, I told him softly, my love, my face on his blood-soaked shirt, kissing away his blood. Relieved. So relieved! My grandmother was killed by the husband whom she hated, I don't know whether I've told you: these sessions get mixed up with each other, become a blur in my memory. They fuse into one another.

Fuse?

All I know is that, there, behind me, your body is my only safety. Your lap my only cradle. For the first time I know respect. Balance. They respect me: you listening, your silence despair as soon as affection, by your connivance.

Accepted?

What affection have I known so far? What mother helped me when I gave birth? They called me Emma like my grandmother: what mother's mother?! I was about to die, did you know? I was about to die at birth. They baptized me in a rush and gave me the name Emma.)

"Emma!"

Startled, she runs. The study, in its half-darkness, is a kind of well. The roses are in their vases. The books are lined up on the shelves. With her eyes she follows the smoke from the cigar in the crystal ashtray on the desk. And the hand.

She runs through the halls stumbling over her heavy velvet skirt, her heart wrung out in an immense scream.

The letter. The letter all crumpled in his hand, the hand on the desk.

"Emma!"

She totters a little. A huge dizziness seems to rise from inside her. Thick vomit close to her mouth.

"I am pregnant!"

"What joy," they say. It is Christmas.

Fritters on the platters on the table, honey in the cups, golden slices of cake, wine muffled in the carafes. And the tree abloom

MARIA TERESA HORTA

in red and silver spheres, and tiny bells that tinkle when people walk. The presents are still wrapped, waiting for hurried fingers in their eagerness.

Your closed fingers crush the letter which you have surely just finished reading; your fingers closed in fury and uneasiness. Ease forever lost, just as I wanted it.

    I am pregnant—I say. Look how my belly grows round under my clothes. Am I ready, my mother?

    Oh that pain!
What pain is this what shame! My body ransacked thus against my will. My breasts always under careful modest wraps now brought to the light and my naked legs spread. Blood on the sheets: a little puddle that I try to cover so you will not see it.
What shame!
And she hides her face in the embroidered linen pillowcase. She has not quite understood what just happened, that sudden violence upon her body. Upon her fright-stiffened body. Stiff with fright and disgust she brought her hands toward her thighs and the blood dirtied the tips of her fingers. She looked at them with astonishment.
Repugnance.

    (The first time was with him. On the wedding-night, as custom demands. It was with him. A friend had spoken to me about it, vaguely, giggling, but I could not imagine, Í did not know. All I knew was that I loved him, that his mouth on mine tasted like the pulp of peaches, the juice of ripe peaches. That his hands on my body over my clothes were patient and tender. But when he lay me on the sheets and began to undress me by force, I was visited by an enormous panic. I remembered all the horrible things my friend had told me and before her all my friends at the high school among laughter and sighs and I remembered the noises from my parents' room sometimes at night, my mother's half sobs half sighs of pain and the hoarse noise my father made that frightened me so.

    Fascinated?

EMMA

I began to scream when he opened my legs with unexpectedly harsh, rough hands. I began to scream and he laughed, mocking me, stuffing himself into me with one thrust: huge, monstrous, opening my body, tearing up my belly, killing me as I thought then.

I knew, of course I knew it would happen, but I had not imagined it like that, but like in the books: tenderness mixed with pleasure right away, the very first time. Time spent and not that hurry, that agony. That horror!

And I loved that man, imagine that. And because of that, because I loved him I came to kill him.

Did I kill?
Did I kill?)

She stares ahead, sitting in the rocking chair: straw and matte finish, smooth wood that she strokes softly with her fingers. Automatic.

"The woman you saw yesterday from your window, standing in the square, that was Emma."

She refuses to believe it.

"You will do what I want. The more you rebel against me the more I will enjoy it."

She remembers the smiles, the knowing looks of the others. She is afraid even of her mother. A deep fear that melts into the desire in his eyes.

How he nauseates her! How she hates him!

"Let me! Come on! Let me! You don't want to be mine, but force tastes even better!"

The woman you saw yesterday in the square was Emma.

Emma looks at the square, the pigeons flutter close to the paving stones: centuries-old, cracked stones, greenish with lichen (with slime?); the moisture that the river glues to the walls of the

MARIA TERESA HORTA

houses, to the flagstone floors. To the statue.
In the middle of the small square in front of the house: the statue. A woman dancing, frozen in mid-gesture, a transparent tunic fluttering up her legs, a small tambourine in her left hand, hair thrown back. If one looks at her from up close, very close by, she seems to smile. But the years have eaten away her expression and the woman who leans against the window, with her head against the warm glass, imagines her lost forever within her own sketchy gesture, her eyes fixed in the distance, her legs suddenly arrested.

In the candid photo, Emma lifts her head and looks for her window in the glare of the sun; she walks fast holding in her arms the huge bouquet she has just bought:
Roses.
"Roses, do you remember?"

At dinner she will take a yellow rose from the table and pin it to the low-cut neckline of her white dress, tight around the hips but flowing open with every movement.
Between her breasts, the rose.
Later, the enormous ruby he himself will hang around her neck in the living room, in front of the mirror, everyone looking on while his cold fingers brush her skin.
He knows, Emma thinks: all the details, the minutiae. She turns and smiles, complicitous.
She smiles.
They will notice that I have smiled. They will look at the rose on my chest. But they look at her mirror image, while her husband places the ruby around her neck:

"Merry Christmas, my love."

She goes down the stairs, the hem of her dress brushing the steps, her daughter by the hand going to the park. They will cross the small square, a widening of the road in front of the house and will walk the tree-lined streets in silence.

The girl likes to walk like that by her mother's hand. She much prefers it to riding a horse or a carriage, dozing in the corners, crouching in fear of her mother's fixed gaze. Feverish and determined.

EMMA

"Emma!"

She glides through the hallway, stumbling over her velvet skirts, her heart compressed in a huge scream she does not let out.
The letter. The crumpled letter on the desk.
"He knows all," she thinks.
He knows all.

(Night after night I dream:
my hair is a wing. Does it look like a wing when it moves: dancing?)

Sometimes she wakes up screaming, sitting up in bed, alarming the whole house.
A small cold sweat covers her body, the roots of her hair, her face.
She still screams after she has woken, prey to a dull terror that never leaves her.
That never leaves her: persistent.
He asks, impatient: "what is it, what is it?" and fans her, mildly annoyed at being disturbed.
"This woman is crazy."

he said one of those times with a threat in his voice.
She never remembers her dreams.

Hope?
Trembling, she leans against the door to his office, not daring to look him in the face.
Who is she, after all, to come and disturb him among his books?

"My mother . . ."
"Quiet! Do not try to seduce me into your disobedience. Fulfill your father's will!"

With her finger she runs down her wet breasts, her belly, her pubis, the inside of the body's lips. Underwater, her fingers have a soft asperity that has excited her ever since she was small.

She leans her head against the edge of the bathtub.

And her fingers continue with their enveloping and firm dance, drawing forth a low moan. Closer and closer to the clitoris, touching it lightly and fleeing to hold up and delay the orgasm. Up from below, opening the vagina a little with her other fingers to allow the hot bath water to enter, filling her with a voracious pleasure, lifting up her body, her legs open. But the fingers return to the clitoris and insist, in a slow, soft movement, feeling it big and thick and firm. She tries to stop, delay a little longer, but her entire body explodes not once but two three times in a row, as usual.

Exhausted she closes her eyes and abandons herself to sleep.

Drowsy.

She dreams of the doll that turned and turned waiting for her laughter or her tears. Anything to put an end to the silence between the two finally intact, but only afterwards.
And Emma slides a little deeper into the tub, the water reaches her lips, and her fingers press down on her chest as if to push her down. Far down.
Everything about her is so tender. Suddenly so tender.
Sometimes when she was small and her mother pressed her against herself she felt precisely that same calm.
Security?
That same peace in the soft warmth of her white and sweet body. Smelling like that, of milk.
Her mother's body smelled of milk and candy. Of vanilla. Even now she thinks of how good it would taste, if she were to lick it . . .
Eat her?
She sinks deeper into the tub. Just a little. She swallows the water slowly. She shivers: the water tastes sweetly of soap mixed with the acid of bath salts.
Does it taste of mother?

It tastes of mother: eat her? No. When she was very little she imagined rather that it would be good if her mother swallowed her so she could rest warm and quiet inside of her.

One day her mother had said, kissing her all over and laughing, "I'll eat you all up." And Emma had felt a shiver of pleasure running all along her body.

All along her body.

She begins to choke and is frightened. Very frightened. Quickly she lifts her shoulders and pulls herself up, coughing. Convulsed. Pale as death. Her eyes fill with tears that wander down to her breasts and then lose themselves in the water, which is now almost completely cold.

"Emma!"

She trembles when she sees the doorknob begin to turn. But he gives up almost immediately and only shouts angrily from behind the door "hurry up, you are late."

Indifferent.

She would rather he waited for her in the living room. She would rather he left her alone, far away.

The guests had started arriving when she got up out of the tub and, wrapped in her towel, went to the room, shivering with cold.

A frayed cold from a fever whose cause she does not know.

On the bed, her black dress.

The wrought gold earrings are on the dressing table; the diamond and pearl bracelet that had belonged to her murdered grandmother is still locked in its case inside the jewelry drawer.

It is the first thing Emma puts on, the bracelet, and then she goes to look at herself in the large mirror, framed in old wood, its round feet firmly planted on the floor. She looks at herself very closely.

"Merry Christmas, my dear."

On the table, the fritters and the crepes. Sweet wine in the goblets and candles burning in silver chandeliers and in bronze chandeliers with small griffin heads.

MARIA TERESA HORTA

On the table however, she had ordered that the crystal chandeliers from her grandfather's house be placed: an almost transparent woman holding an amber colored candle high above her head. From the candle holder two large tears hang down, crystal too. They tremble.

In the next room there are small tables with ashtrays, glasses, and a biscuit girl balancing two eggs of different colors, one in each hand.

Childhood balance?

Emma comes down the staircase slowly, hearing with displeasure the noise of people talking and laughing. Above the rest, she hears his voice, clearly. And the lover's voice.

Are they talking to each other?

She thinks of the plan—of her plan—and walks more firmly on her legs which are still weak. She takes a deep breath and pushes open the door.

They all look at her, very pale in her black dress.

They look at her for one second in the silence that has fallen upon the room. She can almost see the silence. Touch it. She flees from it: she laughs aloud.

The spell is broken—she advances with outstretched hands toward her guests.

They say: you look beautiful!

And she knows that the black dress brings out her pallor.

She had planned it.

"She is happy tonight," they think.

Between Emma's breasts nothing but a yellow rose. She had taken it from a jar in the dining room before going up for her bath.

A yellow rose moistened by the warmth of her breasts. And all can see the small dew on it and look at it and immediately look away.

But she shows off. She likes to show off thus naked under the soft satin of the tight dress. The very low cut, the naked arms, the slim legs appearing in the slits that begin at the top of her thighs.

She is aware of eyes on her thighs, on her arms, on her breast. She leans for a moment against the wall before continuing to laugh aloud, going from one group to the next. Indispensable.

The air is warm with the dry wood burning and crackling in the fireplace.

(I am barren, have I ever told you that? At least, he always asserted that I was barren. The doctors never found anything. They said that there was no physiological reason for my not getting pregnant. He would observe, "It seems that you derive some pleasure from your body's refusal," and I laughed to myself, curling up within this disobedience to his will. I never had any pleasure with him, or with any man, for that matter. My mother used to say, "pleasure is something for men," but I had mine. On my body I found it with my own fingers. Every time he raped me, forced me, entered me stiff with rage for my constant refusal. Afterwards I would go into the bathroom and behind the locked door masturbate for hours, coming for myself. When I returned to the bedroom he was asleep naked on the bed and I watched him in the darkness, breathing him till morning, fighting both my passion and my rage. That despair.

That violence.

And my heart would shatter.

How many times have I told you this?—it would shatter and I was a rag, crumpled at his feet. A rag a rag, do you understand?

I would like to see your woman's eyes, hidden behind me.

Protected?

Sometimes I feel this position of superiority is unfair—you can always hear me, see me, your defenses are up.

And what about me? What about me?—I asked him many times, and he would shrug. "But it was a love match," my mother reminded me seeing me feverish and wasted, hatred distilling its fluid into which I plunged whole afternoons, whole mornings fighting a persistent fever, my body shaken with vomiting.

And I vomited afterwards, as if I were vomiting myself, ridding myself of a lethal, but slow poison.

Do you know what fruitfulness is?—do you know what my fruitfulness was? hatred. It was hatred. Hatred is fruitful.

A fruitful space where I burn.)

She stares ahead, sitting in the rocking chair: straw and matte finish, smooth wood that she strokes softly with her fingers; scratching it lightly with her nails, barely touching, prudent, lest a trace be left.

"Prudently. Lest any trace remain of your passage through here. Any vestige."

MARIA TERESA HORTA

She places the roses in the vase: she is a picture of the woman who, in her own house, puts into a vase the roses she had bought; before crossing the small square where the statue of a dancing woman rises is arrested in the transparent air of this winter smelling of chestnuts and burnt grass.—December penetrating her skin, brittle and fine.

She places the roses in the vase: bending lightly, her perfect torso at a slight angle. To be more concrete, she places the roses on the centerpiece of the table, large and round. You pass your fingers over your forehead and shiver. You look around undecided and slide into your favorite chair by the window that looks out onto the small square in front of the house, in the background the river and the grey sky covered with grey clouds heavy with rain that will fall soon washing the woman who plays the tambourine with her hair thrown back and her face lifted where the rain flows and you imagine tears and the large drops that have already begun to beat against the windowpanes through which you look at the woman who stands still in the square below; as if you saw yourself standing there and not in the refuge of your own home.

Where you forget.

You forget.

Gabardine raincoat on your back, you run to the street hair streaming down your shoulders, soaked, face lifted like that of the woman who a short while ago was gazing at your window from the small square in front of the house. And you stop in front of the marble woman and try to tell her laughter from her tears. But the years have eaten away her expression And now leaning against the parapet by the river with your soaked dress clinging to your body you pull the soaking coat closed clutching the fabric with convulsed fingers.

Emma knows she has not much time left.

"Emma!"

"I am ready, mother."

"That's better. In her father's house a girl will obey. As a woman she will obey some day in her husband's house."

Where is the end?
Where is the door?—The threshold, the bridge?

It is the disturbance. Emma knows. The disturbance.

The river has swollen and runs murky from the storm, pecked at by the angry gulls that bite its waters screaming and diving and throwing themselves back into the air through the lines of wind stretched across the town.

"Emma."

I would leave the roses with pleasure and run into your arms. How many minutes will you give me, away from your notebooks, your books, your newspapers?—a world that has always been strange to me and is still forbidden:
"You should be interested in clothes. Leave the books to me. This is how I want you, sweet, and silent. I ask for nothing more than your quiet. Your sweetness . . ."

The cozy house, clothes in the drawers, smelling of lavender, white linen, soft under her fingers, lace cushions on the sofas, the warm silence of the corridors with their sconces that used to burn gas. As in grandmother's time.
As in grandmother's time: Emma stumbles over her high heels when she runs in the dark waiting for his orders. Wishes that she will make sure to fulfill even if she suffers for it.
Even if they disgust her.

(. . . .)

Emma cries. Her blond hair falls down her naked back, moist with sweat, clinging to her neck, to her shoulders, to the marks left by his nails.
She does not dare raise her eyes and look at him. She tries to hide the small puddle of blood spreading on the sheet. She closes her thighs, covered with black marks. She closes them as tight as she can, but he laughs and pries them open again.
She grits her teeth to hold back a scream.

MARIA TERESA HORTA

"What's the harm? He's a man."

Her mother laughs, mocking her. And Emma's heart stops beating for a second. With fear.
Who is it then she can ask for help?

"But it disgusts me."

"You'll push back your disgust. Learn to feign."

Who could help her? She goes back to her embroidery, silent under her mother's watchful gaze.
Can she then never count on anyone? Never?

(. . . .)

With the firm voice of one who knows she has fulfilled her mission, she says, softly. Fearfully:

"I am pregnant. . . ."

What joy, they answer. It is Christmas.

Emma puts on her black, low-cut dress, tight at the waist. She pulls her hair back toward her neck, letting it fall in long curls that hide her face when she bends attentively, attentive to the wishes of her guests. All around, she notices discreetly, the missing glass, wine, cutlery, ashtray. The fruit bowl with the festive arrangement of peaches and flowers.

"How elegant,"

they say.

"So sweet, always glossing over his rudeness and his mistresses that she pretends not to know about. A lady."

By the Christmas tree, Emma. She distributes the gifts one by one. Hers will be the last.

EMMA

All will be looking at her. She pales. Does she totter?

Did she totter, some ask themselves, undecided. Did she totter? In her dress, the rose, and in his hand the ruby shining in the light from the candles and the dull, flickering light of the candelabra smudging the darkness. The setting is sapphires and amethysts, and small diamonds outline the heart cut into the ruby which seems to pulsate with mineral blood. Red heart, engorged with blood, hanging from the nakedness of her neck. (fibrous, brittle)

Hanging from the nakedness of her neck over the more intimate nakedness of her breasts where it seems to become embedded, shivering. And all exclaim with amazement and wonder while before the mirror he fastens the jewel upon her with his cold fingers. A smile on his lips.

And, very pale, Emma also knew that all eyes were fixed on her breasts, precisely on the spot where now the ruby heart shines. And she sees the undisguised irony in his gaze of possession: possession of her too.

Who else will possess her? who else in this obsession of nonexistence. Lost there. And of a sudden she turns, in a panic. She cannot suppress a sigh which, just a little louder, would have been a scream. And all would look at her in surprise:
"How tactless!"

Only a madwoman would scream like that. . . .

Emma knows, she feels a madness taking her over hour by hour. She lets it come, rise, climb along her senses, her nerve fibers.

Emotions immediately restrained. She draws back.

Her husband is waiting for the public expression of gratitude, the public acknowledgment of his generosity.

She bends, waxen as if she were going to fall limp on the rug, her white dress spread out around her. Her blond hair loose down to her still slim waist.

She bends. Who is not hanging upon her gesture? She is the center of all attention.

MARIA TERESA HORTA

"I am pregnant."

I am the center of the world, don't you see? My belly begins to round out perfect under my dresses. Here I am fulfilling the wait for a son. A male son who will follow in his father's footsteps, house and honor.
A name to be passed on from generation to generation.
A lineage from which Emma feels excluded, as she sits embroidering a small cambric camisole.
On the side of the women: spinning their days, smiling and receiving their husbands in their beds and their lovers in the dark of the night.

Her husband waits for the public acknowledgment of his generosity. The recognition. Emma lifts her head by almost nothing and with the tip of her lips kisses him on the mouth; barely touching her husband's mouth, closing her eyes not to see his gaze. Remembering everything, with nausea, unsure of herself and of the reason for this surrender.

(remembering it all)

He will know all. . . . In full detail. And I will be the one to tell him. Who tells him the full detail.
Hope?

I listen to your words:

Why don't you notice me? And why do you leave me to doze for months away from your attention. No more than the attention sufficient to possess me and then you leave or turn your back on me and fall asleep.
Who am I after all, to disturb you, take you from your books, your newspapers, your work? I who do nothing in this houseful of servants and lace, silver, lilacs in the vases, fruit on the table and cakes. On my own, mornings and afternoons, and I said to you, do you remember? let me leave the house and find out what I want. It is no evil, no sin, to earn money. I suffer in these rooms, in this sleepy luxury. In this stagnation of body and soul and you hit me, threw me on the bed and I screamed and the servants began to hover worriedly around the bedroom door and you yelled at them to go and yelled at me in your fury:

EMMA

"I did not marry you so you would go to earn a living as if I could not support you. I am rich. You have all you want, don't you? Do you need more money?"
And you took your wallet out of your coat pocket and started stacking the bills on the small marble table near the door. You did not even count them: a small stack left there after you had gone. And then I left, with the money in the suitcase. Ready for I don't know what.

(I drank a lot and then I would vomit. He said that I must be pregnant. I laughed. I laughed in his face and told him I had drunk. But he did not want to believe it because I never showed. I drank in peace when he was not home. I was discreet.
Quiet.
Do you think some day I will have peace? Maybe that was why I came to you. That I come here every three days, three days a week lying on this divan.
Will I know rest. Will I know peace? when I buried the knife in his neck I did not feel anything but when I saw him fallen on the rug a great happiness came over me.
Relief.
Do you think I am a monster? I know that over there, behind me, you cannot have or make value judgments, but when I leave I continue to think about you. To feel you. And to wish that you felt for me.
Liked me.
Loved me?
The books speak of transference—but I never imagined it would be like this happiness. And this pain.
Simultaneously.
I ask myself: had I known, would I have come?
You have now taken his place.
My mother's?)

"The woman you saw from the window yesterday, standing in the square, that was Emma."
The first time the voice addressed her, she acted as if she had not heard it.

She arrives home. After the divan, the rocking chair. There is a difference—at home she is alone: no one behind her to listen, to hold her when she falls.

She sits in her corner by the tall window that looks upon the river. She had dismissed the servants, pushed her mother out of the house. She has to find herself alone.

All has to be re-imagined: different endings differences for her life; ways in which all could have happened.

For instance:

Death.

In her hand, the knife with which he cut the pages of books, holding it in the closed fingers—wrist.

"Emma!"

Startled, she runs. The study in semi-darkness, like a kind of well. The flowers are in their vases, the books lined up on the shelves that cover almost all the wall space. In the small spaces left bare by the books, two pictures where women evanesce as if dissolved like the smoke of ever dimmer memories of a past lived centuries ago.

She particularly likes one of a woman looking steadily ahead of her while under, inside her face another woman's face seems to occupy a space—still behind her skin, dilute, fluid but breaking out a little.

She stands beside the picture. With her eyes she follows the path of the smoke from his cigarette in the heavy ashtray on the desk. And his hand.

The letter is there, crushed, then straightened again then crushed harder; crushed in the hand on the waxed top of the desk. Beside it the small sharp paper knife. For opening books and letters.

"Whore!"

Emma recoils. Or rather, she thinks she recoils but finally she advances. She goes ahead with her plan; she stops—does she totter?

He knows all, the details. I described them minutely in the letter:

EMMA

The breasts that the other one licked, the moans, the thighs driven crazy by his mouth, his spittle on her shoulders, the skin under my arms swollen by long sucking.
The swollen, sucked clitoris.
He knows all.
All of what? All?

"Bitch!"

She advances, dragging her feet on the dark grey carpeting—does she totter?

. . . the black satin dress molding her body, covering her feet, tight in the waist, the yellow rose in her decolletage, the heart-cut ruby bloodying her breast. Chilling the blood in her breast.
She totters—the guests suspect she does, watching her walk around the room smiling always, attentive.
She moves forward softly, her eyes full of tears, staring at the hand that clutches the sheet of paper she knows so well. And her own hand, extended as if she wanted to lean against the heavy mahogany desk for support, ready, however, to glide toward the freshly sharpened knife.
He grabs her suddenly in a fury, silent, cold. His icy fingers press her neck firmly.
At first Emma does not struggle, does not feel anything, does not desire anything. But her hand, still gliding along the desk, is already clutching the knife so it hurts. She does not know when or how she raises the knife and plunges the sharp blade into his throat.
The surprise; the surprise—she will forever remember her husband's eyes. There was a convulsive movement and the heavy body fell on her while his hands opened and let her go.
She supports him; she forgets that she herself is still choking, coughing, the air cannot pass through the swollen, aching throat he would have torn, broken without mercy if she had allowed it.
She watches him fall; she kneels, bends over all that thickly bubbling blood. Slowly.
"What a relief," she says, aloud.

Peace?

MARIA TERESA HORTA

She stares ahead, sitting in the rocking chair: straw and matte finish, smooth wood that she strokes softly with her fingers; scratching it lightly with her nails, barely touching, prudent, lest a trace be left.

"Prudently. Lest any trace remain of your passage through here. Any vestige."

Translated by Renata R. Mautner Wasserman

SWEET MARMALADE, SOUR ORANGES

(excerpt)

by

Olga Gonçalves

OLGA GONÇALVES

Olga Gonçalves was born in Angola, the daughter of well-to-do Portuguese colonials; she was educated in Portugal and at the University of London. Since the colony's independence Gonçalves has chosen to make her home in Lisbon where she earns a modest but satisfying living teaching English part-time to the employees of a private company.

Gonçalves began her literary career as a poet, publishing her first book in 1972, and after the Revolution—because of the Revolution—turned to fiction. As she explained to an interviewer: "The Revolution took place and I lost all my property in Angola. Finding myself alone and penniless, I decided to make a 180 degree turn. I thought: how can I participate in what is happening in the country? I can not continue to write subjective poetry; I decided to write novels" (interview with Fernando Dacosta, Jornal de Letras*). She was awarded the prestigious Ricardo Malheiro Prize for the first of these,* A Floresta em Bremerhaven *(*The Forest in Bremerhaven, 1975*).*

*Olga Gonçalves's novels do indeed participate in the reality of contemporary Portugal whether they be the testimonial novels that recreate the experience of the Portuguese workforce in France and Germany or the novels that explore the situation of upper-middle-class youth and their response to the disintegration of the family in that segment of society. Her novels are a commitment to society, which they reproduce from a historical, a sociological, and a linguistic point of view. Gonçalves spent the 1980-1981 academic year at the National Humanities Research Center at Triangle Park, North Carolina, as the recipient of a grant from the Tinker Foundation, writing a novel on the aftermath of the Revolution (*Ora Esguardae, 1982*). An equally interesting product of that year was the critically underrated* O Livro de Olotolilisobi, *a fine poetic diary in which the author records her heightened self-knowledge in an ambience that is at once alien and appealing. Writing—fiction in particular—is for her a form of knowledge: "Fiction is our capacity to dream, to love; it is fiction that brings out of hiding all that we do not know."*

Stylistically, Olga Gonçalves's fiction is characterized by a fidelity to oral speech, by her extraordinary ability to capture the linguistic idiosyncracies of all levels of society. It is this characteristic that makes some of her work exceedingly difficult to translate. The following selection from Mandei-lhe uma Boca, also published as a story in the journal Colóquio Letras, exemplifies Gonçalves's ability to record speech and to penetrate the essence of contemporary Portuguese life. In this case, it is the angry tirade of an adolescent female who reacts energetically to, and often rejects, the many stimuli in her personal and family lives.

Works by Olga Gonçalves

Poetry

Movimento, *1972*
25 Composições e 11 Provas de Artista, *1973*
Só de Amor, *1975*
Três Poetas, *1981*
Caixa Inglesa, *1983*
O Livro de Olotolilisobi, *1983*

Fiction

A Floresta em Bremerhaven, *1975*
Mandei-lhe uma Boca, *1977*
Este Verão o Imigrante Là-Bas, *1978*
Ora Esguardae, *1982*
Rudolfo, *1985*
Sara, *1986*
Armandina e Luciano, o Traficante de Canários, *1988*
Contar de Subversão-Romance, *1990*

SWEET MARMALADE, SOUR ORANGES

Tell me. Do parents end up tired of their children or do they not? In short, are we or are we not a big drag? I can even understand why my father doesn't mind taking that other one's kid to the zoo. Don't you see why? It's easy to see. At least it changes his problem. And, since it is just the beginning, he doesn't even feel the pressure. No, he doesn't feel it. And he's a long way off from us. But I wouldn't say that he has forgotten, who says that? And if he wants to forget us, let him. I don't like people to go out of their way for me. Period. I'm not a child. I can take care of myself. Let me turn twenty-one and then you'll see. I said I'd do it and I will. I guarantee it. I'm fed up with living with people. I'm fed up. Period. Because I am. Living with other people I can't really do what I want. A for instance? Look, walking around the house naked. Candida would faint right on the spot. Eat when I want to. Listen to records as loud as I want

---

From *Mandei-lhe uma Boca* (*Sweet Marmalade, Sour Oranges*), by Olga Gonçalves (Lisbon: Caminho, 1977).

to. Only when I play my records do they remember that loud music bothers them. It's one of the crazy things about that house. And that's not all. If I lived alone I'd know who phoned me. Or I would be home and would answer myself, or if I were out and didn't answer, they would call me again. It's just that nobody gives me my telephone messages. Never. No matter how often I ask my sister, my brother, everybody, they forget. Not to mention Candida, because that one scares everybody. For instance, if it's a guy, she gives him short shrift: "Little Miss Sarah is not in and I don't know if she'll come home for dinner. I don't even know if I will see her today." Then she hangs up before he can even leave a message. And she mixes up all the names! What screw-ups! I've lost a lot of messages, people I was interested in, and I never even found out that they called me. Once I even glued a pad to the telephone table. Do you think anybody paid any attention? No way. It never bothered them. The pad just flew out of there. But who could have done it? It hits you right in the eyes—either Candida or my mother. Or maybe even the two of them. It was ruining mama's little inlaid table. The one it took years to find at Antonio João Madeira's on the Road to the Polytechnical School. I know all their names. "My dear Mitninszki!" "Oh, lamps, Calas makes very good ones! It's too bad he's so slow." Mitninszki went off to Rio. What hatred! That mother of mine is a real production! It takes tons and tons of patience just to put up with her! How did it come about, you and her? Your fathers were friends, weren't they? As girls you used to go together to the zoo to learn how to roller skate. I know that. It seems that you always wanted to go very fast, and what falls you'd take! My mother told me. Both of you would skate-dance with that mulatto teacher. You know, he's still alive, he's still there. The little kids still go there to skate with him. I know. It's not that I go there, but there are certain things I know. My poor mother, she's a good person. And yet, sometimes. In May, for example, it wasn't a bit funny. I needed her so much. I didn't know yet if I would be taking exams. I asked her not to leave Lisbon. You think she listened to me? Fat chance. Well, there you have it. All right, she was exhausted. That's well and good. But she went about her own business. You think she would put off going out of the country with her little group, or whoever she went with? And do you think she wrote to me? What? What the heck are you saying? As if anything was ever taken care by phone? We know what the telephone is like. It's all shouting. "Are you there?"—"Yes, Is this you, mother?"—"Yes. How are you?"—"Fine, we're fine. And you, mother?"—"Listen, is your father around?"— "No. How's your trip?"—"Good. Listen, we mustn't talk too long!"—"Listen, mom!"—"Well, good bye, we mustn't stay on any longer!"—"Good bye, mother! Love and kisses!"—"Lots of kisses!" That's the telephone bullshit. And I told her so. I told my mother so. And that my notion is that she did a pretty good job of worming her way out of dealing with all the troubles she thinks we give her. You know—me, Xana, Rosarinho, my father, the whole family. But to tell you the truth, you think it bothered me that she went away? It bothered me at the time, that's true. I even cried. But when you look at it, it was good she went away. Why, she was finally being truthful! She did what she felt like doing. Period. No faking. You know what else? It's always the same story. What bothers me so much is all that faking. And that's everybody. Everybody. Look at my grandfather. My grandfather, always the madman, but when he comes through the door no one knows how to behave they're so scared they might upset His Highness. Not even my grandmother. He takes ages to wipe his glasses, ages to position himself on the sofa so he can watch TV. All this contributes to his well-being. Because he never had to work. His family was rich. He's furious over the Revolution. Come to think of it, I must be worse than the Revolution for him. Yes, I answer back. Well! I get so angry. Sometimes I tell him off. There's nothing I won't tell him. But don't you see that what he is, is a great fake, with all that bowing around my grandmother, wearing her down finally with all that penny-pinching. The only thing that saves her is her "Fernandinhos" tea and the sewing she does for the Sisters of Saint Vincent de Paul. What lives they lead. And what a madman he's been. Don't you know? Oh, I bet you know. Now he doesn't even fool around, the poor thing. That is, he still fools around, but only as a type of voyeur. You're laughing? He goes to peep, and then pay. Look, everybody in the family knows it. My uncles and aunts laugh like fools. He keeps an apartment to take girls to. Someday I'd like to disguise myself and go to one of those coffee-shops where he goes to

SWEET MARMALADE, SOUR ORANGES

meet them. What a gas. Dark glasses, a wig, boy would I disguise myself. I'd unmask him in front of the entire family. Maybe then he would leave off his moral preaching once and for all. My God. Just thinking about it! How sweet. It would beat everything. My word, I'd still like to pull off this prank. Boy, would I. He's fond of saying: "Search your conscience!" Ah, I can't. I can't stand that—looking into your conscience. Always laying down rules, always giving orders. Jesus. If I ever get to live alone, I still won't believe it. All my troubles will be over. I wouldn't set aside a day for visiting my family. Let me turn twenty-one and you'll see. I've already got my apartment. It's rented, but it can be unrented. My mother? I don't know. We still don't know if she's coming home for Christmas or staying on in Crans sur Sierre. No, I don't know if her nerves are better. Daddy has the key to the mailbox and Xana has the other one. She must have written but I haven't seen Daddy to know for sure. What a crashing bore Christmas is! The whole family gathered, and all the little gifts. All of it falsely showing that everybody's happy. Sure, I'm not saying that it couldn't be all right, but you don't do it by setting up people who can't stand each other and who have to talk themselves into being there and show off their happiness. Who knows about my mother. Maybe she won't even come. Only yesterday I kept my eyes peeled for my father until after three a.m. to ask him about it, but I ended up falling asleep and didn't hear him come in. As it happened I was so bummed out, like really bummed, you know. And I turned myself on. Did I get stoned! Well, as a rule, I don't do it. When I turn on it's always with a group for fun. But yesterday, I don't know what was wrong with me. Was I down. My mother! Maybe she got to the point where she didn't care, don't you think? If she's really sick, she won't even give Christmas a thought. I'm so down in the dumps. And school. If there are teachers, there are no students; if there are students, there are no teachers. After the Revolution we all flipped out. Soon it will be Christmas. There are times when time flies by like the wind. It's really something. And at the same time it's a good thing when you want it to zip by, that is. But now, maybe because I'm waiting around, time seems to drag so much, you know? I don't know if I'm at the end of my rope. Yeh, I'm going to stay calm. Stay calm. No thanks. I have a handkerchief in my bag. Thanks.

I'm a fool. Whew. Probably the only thing that could make me laugh today would be a letter from Diogo. So everything could be talked out, at last. Because he never wanted to talk to me. Maybe, because he was really mad. Or may be he thought I was some airhead bimbo. Or maybe he takes me for some little kid. That's all right. I was sixteen. But listen. I'd already been around the block. Why can't I get this out of my head? Sometimes I'd like to sit down and write to him, but I just let the months slip by, and now it's too late. And his father was one of the ones who slipped off to Brazil. He took his wife and kids. Except George, of course. Boy, do I hate his father. Because, just because. I have two friends who write to Diogo. Yes, he's golden, he can get along anywhere. Some of the Portuguese got big jobs over there. Sure, people like Diogo's father. I'm really antsy about next summer. Maybe at least his son will come to visit. I didn't see them showing up this year. He'll probably go to Moledo. If he does come he's sure to stay in his grandparents' house. No. Across from Antonio Pedro's house. Across the street? No, not across the street. They have a place. But I got it all wrong. I meant to say in back of Antonio Pedro's house. You knew him, didn't you? You were in his house, weren't you? Not I, but I, too, noticed that tree. What? An Araucária, maybe? I'm not sure I like it, but I always give it a good look when I go by. They told me that every year a whole new set of branches appear. It's gotten really big. My father tells me that when he was a kid he used to ride around there on his bicycle and that the girls used to skate on the asphalt all the way from that place to the Pinhal do Camarido. Imagine that. On the asphalt, no less. It must have been real smooth, don't you think? Riva, you were there only once? But you must remember the little chapel up ahead, a miniscule chapel, always neatly whitewashed, they called the "Little Souls"? Just imagine, they used to skate all the way to the chapel. Nobody goes over there these days. It's called the old road. Now there's the new road. It's neat. In those days Moledo must have been so boring! Even if they say those were the good old days. When there were only a few people and a half dozen shacks—nothing else. Ancora was where the ranchers went. Moledo was more select. Don't tell that to my father and my grandparents. My grandparents used to go to the Pension Flora.

SWEET MARMALADE, SOUR ORANGES

It's still there. Still there. It's great, clean as a whistle, and the service is beautiful. It was later on they built their house. Imagine, there wasn't even the Club yet or tennis. For dancing there were only the "verbenas" in Monção or Caminha or out in the villages. In Gondarém, it seems. It seems, too, that they picnicked on the Ilha dos Amores. And to Insua. Every fifty years or so there's a great drought, and all the people from that area go there. They bring their oxcarts and everything. They carry knapsacks. There's a procession. Honoring Our Lady of Insua, the statue is in the chapel belonging to the fort. My father always says it's a shame the whole thing is so deserted. But the funniest part are those poor people—the ordinary people, you know, the Joe Blows—believing that the drought is a miracle. They look wide-eyed and say that the waters have parted just to let them pass through. Whew. I can't stand it. I laugh my head off.
Apparently the priest does not disabuse them of the notion, he just lets them wallow in their holy foolishness. You should see my father get furious over this and arguing with my grandparents. Of course my grandparents accepted everything the priest said. What was needed was to beef up the people's faith. My father would counter that what they needed was enlightenment. Every time I think of it! My mother hasn't yet given up "heaven" or "hell" (you can't do anything with her) and my father has no one to help him. Another one of the many problems. Me? I never get into such conversations. Besides, they still treat me sometimes like a baby infant. Infant, maybe because I do not go along with everything. Nothing irritates me more. And the grown-ups? Have they really grown up? Or have they just lived longer? Do they have a better understanding of everything of what's going on around them? And how about what you don't even know is going on, tell me that. What I think is that. It's that we need loads of strength. A lot of courage. It's a good thing there are people who make us laugh. I like to laugh. It makes up for those times when I'm feeling like I've walked into a tunnel, a very long tunnel. It's as dark as can be. I mope around in sadness, a kind of pain here, one that does not go away. It's as if the darkness rose up through my entire body, and I wasn't even able to see, let alone understand what was going on outside. That's to say, not even being able to imagine, you know? Dream. Make plans. That's the way I was today. And

OLGA GONÇALVES

that's why I thought of coming to see you. To tell you the truth, I missed yoga! I didn't go! No way could I concentrate today. There's so much going on in my head. We'll see if Diogo comes back next summer. I'm looking around for information. But we still have to get through Christmas. How? No, there's nothing I have to do tomorrow, I have no plans. It's Saturday, but I have no plans. I was just going to the hairdresser. Marmalade? Oh, that sweet stuff, that sweet stuff made from bitter oranges. I never made the stuff, but do you want me to stay around and help? I'll stay. It'll even be fun. At home the one who's in charge of the sweets is Candida. All we're good for is emptying jars. I'll help you. I'm even going to find it fun. Yes, I've already noticed that you've got a cold. Oh, the oranges are cut up the night before? It's only ten minutes to midnight. We can still do that today. What a shame! You cut them up this morning? I know, I know you don't like to go to bed late. My mother always says that you picked up that habit in England. But it's just that for us midnight is so early. It's very late over there? God! Those people don't have lives! What a bother, going to bed so early. And you really liked living there that much? For our bunch, London is shopping, clothes, Carnaby Street, and King's Road! Will we make the marmalade tomorrow? If you want to, you can even explain everything to me and I'll do it all. I just said that. It's O.K. We'll do it together. I guess you think it's time for bed, huh? I'll sleep on this couch. I'll sleep like a baby. It's so fluffy and big. I'll make it up. Give me the bedclothes. I'll make the bed. O.K. then the two of us will make it. I like flowered sheets. My mother bought me some Mary Quants. The bottom sheet is plain—cyclamen—and it's of a single color. The top one and the big pillows are flowered cyclamen, rose and white. They are enough to drive you crazy. The eiderdown will do. It's warm in the room. Can I still listen to some records, if I play them softly? I have everything, everything. I don't need anything. A kiss. Good night. What's going on? Oh, I know who you are calling. Are you calling Candida? You're going to tell her I'm sleeping over, aren't you? Ask her if my father came home for dinner. Listen, ask her if he said anything about my mother.

Translated by George Monteiro

THE DAY OF THE MARVELS

(excerpt)

by

Lídia Jorge

LÍDIA JORGE

Virtually unknown at the time of the Revolution of 1974, with her first novel Lídia Jorge became one of the dominant figures on the Portuguese literary scene. Born in Boliqueme, a small village in the Algarve, in 1946, she made her way to Lisbon to study Romance Philology and became a secondary school teacher, first in Angola and Mozambique. She then returned to Lisbon to continue her teaching and to embark on the career as a writer that has won her several important prizes and recognition on both sides of the Atlantic.

As of 1988, Lídia Jorge had published four novels. The distinguishing features of this work are a concern with historical circumstance and social change in Portugal and Portuguese-speaking Africa; a kinship with the Latin American writers García Márquez and Vargas Llosa; and a preoccupation with the reproduction of orality. Her first novel, O Dia dos Prodígios *(The Day of the Marvels, 1980), has had numerous editions in Portugal and Brazil. It has been labelled by the distinguished critic Eduardo Lourenço as one of the two* livros-chave *(key works) of the Revolution, which Jorge approaches in a magic realist vein reminiscent of Gabriel García Márquez's* One Hundred Years of Solitude. *Her next novel,* O Cais das Merendas *(The Snack Wharf, 1982), sets aside magic realism but continues to explore Portugal's social problems, this time, the issue of cultural colonization, particularly evident in her native Algarve. The result is a metaphorical representation of a society in transition, if not in disintegration. In her third novel,* Notícia da Cidade Silvestre *(Notes from the Urban Jungle, 1984), Jorge narrows her focus to the developmental experience of women, creating to that end two remarkable female characters who rub off on each other much like Don Quixote and Sancho, as they make their way through the urban jungle. In* A Costa dos Murmúrios *(The Whispering Coast, 1988) she returns to the bigger picture, this time the pre-Revolutionary past and the horrors of the colonial war in Africa. Lídia Jorge does not speak of* herself as a feminist but it is clear that although only one of these novels deals predominantly with women's lives, the latter are never far from her mind as she works.

The selection translated here—a fine example of Jorge's recreation of orality—is taken from O Dia dos Prodígios, *a novel that records brilliantly what Jorge perceives to be the failure of the Revolution. The protagonist of the novel is a collective rather than a person: a rural community lost in the hinterlands of what appears to be the Algarve. The principal figures in the fragment are Macário, a singer who suffers from unrequited love; his friend, World War I veteran Manuel Gertrudes; and the town busy-body, Jesuina Palha. The scene is the sudden arrival of the long-awaited "revolution" in the form of a truckload of Maoist soldiers and an equally sudden departure that leaves the villagers untouched. The Revolution remains a remote "marvel" far less real to them than the prodigious snake that had appeared to them a year earlier.*

Works by Lídia Jorge

O Dia dos Prodígios, *1980*
O Cais das Merendas, *1982*
Notícia da Cidade Silvestre, *1984*
A Costa dos Murmúrios, *1988*
A Última Dona, *1992*

THE DAY OF THE MARVELS

Matilde spoke. The days go by so slowly while we wait. And João Martins spoke. But the years always go by fast. Just yesterday I was a boy, with fuzz on my lip. And Manuel Gertrudes spoke. When I remember the war, I could swear it was yesterday. I remember everything. The things I saw, the thoughts I had. Ah, but if I want to remember what I saw and ate this morning, I think an eternity has passed between that moment and the present. And Lourenço spoke. Stop talking about the origins of time, it always brings on bad thoughts. And Matilde spoke. Sometimes it even brings on your confusion. And Manuel Gertrudes spoke. That's right. Especially when two people remember the same thing. And the mule driver spoke. Yes, and one says it was in '36 and the other in '39. And João Martins spoke. You're so quiet, Macário, say something. And Matilde spoke. It's that he's waiting for two things to happen,

---

From *O Dia dos Prodígios* (*The Day of the Marvels*), by Lídia Jorge (Lisbon: Europa América, 1980).

THE DAY OF THE MARVELS

the first maybe as impossible as the second. And Manuel Gertrudes spoke. The second we're all waiting for. The first only he's waiting for, like never before. Remember everybody, that since the afternoon the sergeant killed the dog, never again has His Majesty come here to sit his ass. Excuse my language. In that canvas chair. He left. And Tiago spoke. That's why the second wait is harder than the first, and involves everybody. It's time to give up hope. The visitors can go fuck themselves, if they come they come. Goddamn.

Macário, as if he wanted to lighten his heart, lifted one leg and began the songs. We have the whole afternoon, folks. Today this may not end. The neighbors sensed that the concrete shadow could begin to reach the street, in spite of its slowness, and so they sat in a line on the stone bench. Macário with his leg lifted in the doorway, resting his foot on the seat of a chair. He plucked lightly, with a vibrato, the melody breaking apart like sobs. That one and that one still, and still another like the first. Tiago thought, seeing the reed vibrate the strings, that the instrument might break. He followed all of the movements of the hand. And he felt envy, mixed with longing for another world, where he himself would have been able to pluck music on a sound-box. And those thoughts were sad. They came during and at the very end of that trill, vibrant and ringing, without one word. To him his neighbor's mandolin portrayed women who never complained, nor lost their teeth, and who yet loved much and well. Women who died standing and didn't let themselves be seen being buried. So as not to leave their lovers with the memory of the disfiguration. That was why he had to say, excuse me. Macário stopped, and Tiago spoke. One minute, friend, one minute. Change the tune, this one makes my sight cloud up. Or is it the heat? So Macário concentrated all his effort in a final smile, closed his eyes, let shine his teeth and the whole cavity of his mouth and began to sing also. His whole body swaying. Because of a little snake. Crushed on the ground like the ants. All the people in the village. Ai all the people. Were shitting in their pants. At that moment the children arrived, lured by the music and the singing, with solemn step and their hats off, and the singer repeated the quatrain with his leg in the air. At the end of the couplet, he shut his eyes completely and put his feet together. He raised the mandolin in the air and

spoke. Everything. Everything I sing and play comes right from here. Pointing at his head with his finger.
"You compose well, son. But you're lost in this land." Said Manuel Gertrudes.
They're all mine and I make them up as I go along. Because the listeners were many and approached slowly so as not to interrupt, Macário added another stroke swelling with sound. That rascal from the fields. Thick around as a penny. Lived in all the houses. Ai awaiting an opportunity. And they all spoke. Ai awaiting an opportunity. With dignified enthusiasm. Ai awaiting an opportunity. Macário thanked them, letting the neighborhood chant alone. And he swept the top of his head toward his knees. His hair loose like dark grass to be mown. When Jesuína Palha spoke. What am I seeing, my God? A car is coming. A heavenly car. Heavenly. It's bringing the angels and the archangels. Oh friends. And St. Vincent is driving. Said Jesuína Palha, returning from harvesting with her apron and handkerchief full of the thorny beards of corn. Everyone looked. To be sure, at the bend in the road, on the side where the sun sets, appeared something so extravagant that everyone who managed to make out the blotch of colors, turning his head, thought he would fall flat on his face in the street. Though the blot, already voluminous, approached slowly. Occupying in space the three dimensions of something visible, solid and palpable. But the men, putting a hand to their brow, and making a great effort to see clearly what approached with such majesty, spoke. They were now less hasty and more lucid. Yes, we are. We're going to be visited by beings that came out of the sky, that come from other spheres. Where the centuries belong to another age. Keep away, neighbors, a sight of this can kill. The children ran out onto the road, spurred by courage. They felt that the sea was going to arrive behind a boat with floating whitish sails, unfurled in the very light breeze of the afternoon. And they also began to gesture excitedly with their arms, sketching swimming motions. But Macário. Having been the last to perceive, he saw exactly. At the moment of the surprise he still had his eyes closed repeating for the last time. Awaiting an opportunity. Awaiting an opportunity.
   This is a combat vehicle. Oh neighbors. In truth, right in the middle of the road advanced a singular car, singular because it

THE DAY OF THE MARVELS

came full of gallant and epic soldiers, already invading the center of Vilamaninhos with flags and flowers. And they sang by way of a loudspeaker as if they came supplied with a powerful orchestra. Now the spectacle was already so real and beautiful that everybody. Having forgotten those first seconds of astonishment and confusion. They felt touch, song, and hearing had been suspended a long time ago. So that they only hear and see that which was arriving on top of an open armored car. Everybody was sure that since the time of the kings nothing like this had been seen. Ah what a marvel. Then the car stopped in front of the group, and there was a moment of silence so solemn that people thought they were going to die. But a soldier. Particularly handsome, having no doubt been born in a very different land. He began to speak from atop the car, now stopped in the square. He said things. That there had been a re vo lu tion, and that it was necessary to liven up. Because everything. Everything. And he opened the arms of a saviour. Everything was going to be changed. He spoke so well, that everybody found himself enchanted by the tone of that voice. And by the masculine manners, being nevertheless delicate, as if the soldier didn't feel the weight of his body. By the uniform, by the hair lightly curled. And no one was able to say whatever it was he was going to, prisoners all of the surprise and the marvel. Not even Macário. Not even Manuel Gertrudes. The other soldiers, feeling no doubt the turmoil invading the natives of Vilamaninhos, lifted their arms and said what the listeners perhaps wanted to say. But the soldiers spoke as a group. So loud and vibrant. That the Vilamaninhenses understood only that they had said a great thing, and that they would have still greater things to say in the future. When they finished the square was full of people listening. One didn't even feel the void of those who were absent. And Macário, fearing that the inhabitants of Vilamaninhos were playing the role of drunks to perfection, and excited, because before the arrival, he had heard from the mouth of his neighbor, that his place ought not be there. Feeling himself the countryman of those strangers. He spoke.

"We here knew very quickly, two days after, that you had fought the revolution. But we never thought we'd get to see the heroes."

The soldier who had spoken raised a hand in thanks. All the

others had a solemn and martial air, no one doubting that such men would win the greatest battles. The very handsome soldier, with flowers shedding in his buttonholes, also spoke. It was necessary that that region convince itself that the time of freedom had arrived. The less indolent women, and the girls, who had been the last to come down, but now found themselves closest to the vehicle of war, began to feel that they couldn't repress their spontaneous feelings any longer, and because the spectacle was the most enchanting of their lives, began to shout all the words of enthusiasm they knew. They said hellos. Friends, sweethearts, brothers. Divine beings, liberators from hunger and envy. They said angels, beauties, darlings, and visitors. Sirs. And there were those who cried and crossed their arms over their breasts as if they were embracing the soldiers who remained heroic and uniformed on the green car the color of garlic mustard. Singularly open and armored. Manuel Gertrudes dared to speak. I was a soldier. He you see here. And he struck his chest. The soldiers who heard him put a hand to their berets, high up atop the car. And Manuel Gertrudes went on, having loosed his tongue. In this land, since some time ago until now there haven't been any soldiers. They fled at fifteen, afraid that the police would come on horseback looking for them to force them to become soldiers. However I went from '14 to '18, and I never regretted it, in spite of the hardships of the war. Oh friends. The soldier spoke again. Saying. Now. Now the injustices will be repaired. The public treasury distributed equally to all. Because we are driven by an i de al. Adopted by many people. And we are capable of giving our lives for this theory. Look. The neighbors came closer to see, however, one of the soldiers wielded a long object, and the natives, and those who had settled in Vilamaninhos, found themselves obliged to withdraw a few steps. They thought that the afternoon was very full of events, and that still they were going to see right there a show of fire and force. And the first soldier said, while the second untied the supposed weapon, which was bound. That they were going to exhibit that picture before everyone, because they believed. Oh friends. That this was the hour of the humiliated and the oppressed. And who are they? Asked Manuel Gertrudes. Who are they? And the soldier stuffed up his chest You. You. They are you. He repeated. Without you knowing it.

THE DAY OF THE MARVELS

But the future is now called the present. It's enough for all of us to put our faith in the right values. You. Our partners. Springboard for the marvels. Said the soldier, who because he was speaking and moving his hands, seemed more gallant. The girls squeezed their throats with their fingers. Otherwise they would let out indiscreet sighs. And Manuel Gertrudes, with his tongue loosed, said still more. Us? How can you call us that? If we already let the snakes come down into our houses? Wherever there's a villager living, you can still manage to chase the crawling beasts away by burning things. But in the emigrants' houses, in the hot hours, they hiss and lay eggs. In response the soldier said. Look at the picture first. The second soldier unrolled the object which didn't wrap any weapon after all. With a noise of cloth stretched over glue and paper, all that fell out was a strip of wood at the end of a banner. Look. Said the soldier. And everyone could see. It was the very big picture of a man's face, the color of a poppy, with the eyes almost closed in a squint, looking beyond the rectangle of cloth where they had put him. He had broad temples and a pointed beard, made with the point of a little paint brush, which divulged a solemn air as if spreading a good smell. Manuel Gertrudes stammered with emotion at the size of the banner. And he spoke. He looks like Macário, if Macário would comb his hair and take better care of himself. The soldier smiled. No. With a pause. He can't look like anybody, because he was in charge of a great nation, and taught the paths of the real tru th. To everybody. He spoke with vehement gestures, the soldier. And according to what you said he died? Asked Jesuína Palha. Yes, he died. He died for justice. And Jesuína Palha, having forgotten the thorny beards of corn which tortured her skin, said, resolute. Oh shoot! If he died for justice and truth, this one here, it's St. Francis Xavier, because only that one is remembered for having given his word of honor in the Orient. Or Egas Moniz. Said Manuel Gertrudes. Because that one also did what he promised. After all our history is full of great figures. All the children have to do is open the book and it talks about them. But I still say that that one there looks like this one. Pointing at Macário. And the soldier with a big smile of kindness and much sweetness, with the knowing gaze of an expert marksman, and the strong arms of a hero. He said. Friends. This one was born a long ways from here, and he only

LÍDIA JORGE

has to do with our history from these days onward. These. If the time we have were ours, we would tell you why. But today we have to be on our way. And he gave an order to wrap up the picture. You seem pure, good, but ignorant of a lot of things. Said the soldier as if he spoke to children. Did anyone present learn about the roundness of the earth? Well then, we must come back. And with another gesture he ordered the car started. The driver of the vehicle, who was also a soldier like all the others, started up the motor. With two loud cracks, of sudden starts, and the wheels cut a few brief turns to the east. As if they were leaving for Faro. But they couldn't advance, because Jesuína Palha, in one jump, put herself in front of them. And said. And the snake? The soldier already seated, and others standing up, but all in their places, didn't understand the word. A snake? What snake? Asked the first, circumspect. And Jesuína insisted. How is it possible that you come by here and don't explain what happened in this land? I won't even mention the other signs, because I see you're in a big hurry, as if we were contaminating your air. But about the snake. It's urgent that you speak. If not, we'll all die with doubt stuck in our throats. The soldiers appeared possessed by true astonishment. And Jesuína looked at them with their eyes wide open, like someone giving or receiving a last pardon. She also perceived that a certain elegance had faded from the soldiers. One heard the gasoline combust inside the metal belly of the big car. And a soldier spoke. Tell us. We came to learn too.

    Jesuína fluffed her skirt and pulled up her socks held up by garters at the crook of the knee. She shook out the thorny beards of corn, put the bag with the scythe on the ground and began. With the impetus of many gestures. That precisely last summer, on a hot day such as that one had been, in the middle of putting the bread in the oven, the paddle extended, and the tray of bread ready, she had heard screams which had seemed to her to be those of someone pursuing a ferocious animal. And she hadn't been wrong. She had dropped the paddle and gone out into the street with a stick in her hand, ready to face whatever it was. At that moment she had seen her neighbors pursuing a snake of many arms' length, and feeling that those present were incapable of confronting the animal as it should be done, Jesuína beat her breasts with both her hands. She threw herself at it and kneaded

THE DAY OF THE MARVELS

it without pity squish squash on the sidewalk until she felt it come apart. But already dead, the rascal had escaped from her hands, and raised itself into the air above everybody's heads. Is that or isn't that the truth, folks. Two wings had come out of its back, a halo of light issuing from the tongue lit up the head, and like that it had gone up into the sky without another soul coming into contact with it. And Jesuína Palha, making her earrings sway from her ears, ten times more virile than a man, beat her chest in front of the soldiers' car and the people now jammed in the door of the tavern. With all the gestures, acting out the scenes. There was a silence, and a soldier proffered a question. At what time did this happen? Jesuína Palha looked at the sky, compared and said. It would be about two in the afternoon, high noon. The first who had spoken from the beginning, also spoke. We're all pleased, because we've noted that in this region people still like miracles. It's already becoming rare. The car withstood a stronger thrust and disappeared behind the last house, vanishing through the carob trees along the road, because the road made a turn to the east, and that disappearance was too sudden for he who had emerged from the torpor of the wait for scarcely a few brief minutes. When one could no longer hear the last sound of the car the color of garlic mustard on the road, and a funereal silence fell over those present, the women thought that the eaves of the house would fall from rot and mold. The men looked at the clouds and judged that the present still had not begun. Every one feeling too old to witness the happening of the future. Us? Springboards of time? Only the children were sure that the sea was humid and lined with soft sea weeds. Waving their arms excitedly. That was why Maria Rebôla, who had been in the center of the circle of the women, and during the enthusiasm had thought about going to José Jorge Júnior's house to get Esperança Teresa and carry her in her arms so she could see the soldiers in the car. They had arrived so suddenly, when they already were almost not expected. She spoke very loudly, to be well heard. Feeling as if she were the queen of the tragedy.

"Ah family. We had a vision."

All those present glanced at one another and felt somewhat ashamed of themselves. The soldiers had rushed off, charged no doubt with taking the vision to other places. They saw. Looking into one another's eyes. That they had gotten stirred up over nothing. But let the group not scatter. Said Tiago. Your songs were going so beautifully. Macário agreed. Thus he lifted a leg, rested on his knee the whole body of the mandolin. Embracing it. And he sang. A snake from the woods. In the last throes of agony. Ai in the last throes of agony. Slipped away. Slipped away. Off to another community. In the air he left feathers. And on the ground little turds. The shit was like a dog's. And the feathers like a bird's. Everyone speaking. And the feathers like a bird's. But the moon was already climbing high and Macário felt that his neighbors had already drunk a cruel dose of dissatisfaction. That afternoon. Eh friends. Crying washes clean the soul and clears the weight from the forehead. Those who came here to show off didn't even get to hear our voices. And Manuel Gertrudes said. Not everybody would have had the patience to hear Palha talk about the snake. On top of everything, with her crossing herself and shaking her ass so much. But Macário pretended not to understand. We should only listen to each other. Not believe in anything outside ourselves. Whenever we open our ears to others, either they kill dogs or raise our hopes. Manuel Gertrudes reprehended him. Be quiet, Macário. Those folk aren't going to regret what little happened. Because little is always better than nothing. And risking one's life, to me, always deserved a tip of the hat. I knew the force of the shrapnel. I'm talking from the inside. That's why it will be better if you sing—to tell the truth—something about love. For example. Macário looked at his neighbors. No one wanted to leave the square in spite of the night. As if they had experienced elation poorly concluded. Macário felt that deeply. And filled with sadness, there before the gathering, he began to compose a very sad love song so that the Vilamaninhenses could cry publicly for one thing, saying it was for another. It was a story of love pledged, betrayed and lied about. And there was a letter, a return and a refusal. Then there was a desire and a silence. A separation. A sigh, a song, a death. But before that an act of martyrdom and an evasion. Linking some couplets to the ends of others, right after, as if Macário feared that the inspiration would fail, the story he left hanging. When he ended, no one had left, neither to eat, nor to sleep. But they remarked that Macário sang for a woman alone, daughter of another woman. Both being absent. And that if that love were really lived, as it seemed

THE DAY OF THE MARVELS

from the words, it would be a tale to cut the heart to ribbons. Oh sad Macário. Tiago against his will felt his eyes become wet, without anyone seeing that the moon had come and gone, round and ruby-red, beautiful big eye up in the heavens.

translated by Naomi Parker

MY STORY, YOUR STORY

(excerpt)

by

Eduarda Dionísio

EDUARDA DIONÍSIO

Eduarda Dionísio, born to a literary-minded Lisbon family in 1946, earned a degree in Romance Philology and became a secondary school teacher. At the same time, she assumed an active role in the theater and art circles of Lisbon. She has had individual and group exhibits; she founded the Contra Regra theater group and worked with Grupo de Teatro Bando. She was also co-founder of the journal Crítica. *Her greatest success, however, has been in literature, where she is without doubt one of the most powerful witnesses to her own generation.*

Dionísio has published five novels since 1972. Retrato dum Amigo Enquanto Falo *(*My Story, Your Story, *1979) was praised by the distinguished critic Eduardo Lourenço as one of the best novels of the Revolution along with Lídia Jorge's* O Dia dos Prodígios. *All of her novels to date share certain thematic and technical threads. The primary task Dionísio sets for herself is that of transforming into art the political and social experience of her own generation, the effect on that generation of modern Portuguese history with its nearly half a century of dictatorship followed by a peaceful but aborted revolution. Technically, Dionísio has decribed her own work in these terms: "My books are, perhaps, a bit like the description of films that I would like to make; but since I don't have money to make films, I make books"* (Jornal de Letras). *Her interest in film may account for the surface texture of the novels, the interest in detail, in* things, *the many facets of life and culture that constitute the reality of any given historical era. It may also be, though, that this texture is a legacy of the* nouveau roman *with which Dionísio's work has an affinity.*

The selection translated here is from Retrato dum Amigo Enquanto Falo, *a novel composed of discontinuous fragments held together by the persona of the narrator. In considerable detail, the narrator records the experience of her (and Dionísio's) generation: the heady years of underground resistance in the waning years of the dictatorship; the gradual transformation of her group after the Revolution into individuals seduced by material comfort and socio-psychological well-being. The narrator remains at once participant and critic in the socio-political process, maintaining her distance, her integrity, her freedom through writing. Dionísio uses the relationship between the narrator and the friend in the title as the facilitating device that turns political history into fiction at the same time that it allows her to explore the affective, interpersonal dimensions of her generation's experience.*

Works by Eduarda Dionísio

Comente o Seguinte Texto, *1972*
Retrato Dum Amigo Enquanto Falo, *1979*
Histórias, Memórias, Imagens e Mitos Duma Geração Curiosa, *1981*
Pouco Tempo Depois (As Tentações), *1984*
Alguns Lugares Muito Comuns (Diário de uns quantos dias que não abalaram o mundo), *1987*

MY STORY, YOUR STORY

I think that the strangest thing was the convergence of our imaginations and words, swinging towards each other like trapeze artists who never miss while moving from bar to bar, holding each other by the wrists, ankles, even teeth. Our minds and words linked up with the timing of two hands in a carefully practiced piano exercise, or again, like the circus acrobats who take near-fatal plunges, spins, and somersaults but somehow end up on the perch together. As with the famous ones, we didn't have a net between us and the arena below, so the first slip would be the last. Where did the verbal bond, the knowing looks, smiles, and gestures of recognition come from? And the unsigned note I immediately recognized and found amusing, and you, concealing your feelings and saying again the next time we ate together that all love letters are absurd, without even mentioning your own letter (which really didn't amount to much).

From *Retrato Dum Amigo Enquanto Falo* (*My Story, Your Story*), by Eduarda Dionísio (Lisbon: O Armazem das Letras, 1979).

MY STORY, YOUR STORY

They were, after all, just a detail like the scenery in a play.
And I talked almost as if I were going back to those years of the 1970s when napalm was burning up Angola. I was talking as if you had asked me something but you hadn't. You just looked at me, kindly. Something about why I wrote so much during those long years before the fall of the dictatorship when it looked like things would always be the same, stagnant and rotten. Why did I write then?

You're the one who always takes the other side, who goes against the current as Fernando Pessoa says. You, above anyone else, ought to understand this: that everyone had to put on paper what they were thinking no matter how hard it was. Even though, at the same time, it might not make sense to you what one had to go through to produce art that was both political and accessible. But otherwise there was no point in writing.

I wrote a lot and constantly, for days on end, almost without stopping to breathe. It was as if we were living more intensely during that time. And although it wasn't totally a secret activity, it seemed like it was and that I wasn't really reaching anyone, mostly because I was convinced that lining up words on a page more or less mechanically was of little value. I was like those well-meaning activists who continued their struggle in the underground once they left the university scene. But writing was never a choice one made; rather, it was a way of surviving intact, a way of putting into print recent experience you were trying to make sense of and to outline what lay ahead, something I did clumsily and with a lot of guess work.

To know at a given moment whether or not I should go on from my first notebook was a problem: if continuing would mean the dissolution of my consciousness and if every new sentence and page would take me further and further away from involvement. It was a very serious problem, one that obsessed me, but I silenced it because I couldn't explain it to myself very well.

Trying always to write in a straightforward manner so that people could easily understand was exhausting and sad because it became impossible to say the things that I really wanted to say.

I seemed like Penelope in my writing, knitting from a pattern learned in the remote past of childhood, in a style that could be reproduced infinitely.

EDUARDA DIONÍSIO

Or like someone rowing with no clear destination in mind, simply for the pleasure of moving through calm, clear waters, starting out at dawn and finishing at the end of the day only because the sun was setting, I concluded a piece as a notebook ran out and I would just dream up new things until I bought another one.

The inability to emulate the great writers never bothered me. I continued to write because perhaps I thought it was necessary to rescue moments that neither the newspapers nor history books would ever be capable of getting or transmitting with any degree of accuracy.

I tried to compose documents like cave paintings, like Roman stone engravings, or medieval manuscripts—everything very secretly, repressing the pride and the involvement which sometimes came through briefly at the end of a page.

For this reason, details really concerned me, especially adjectives, which often seemed strange to me but which I did not erase because of the respect I had for what was already written; besides, I didn't think it was really made by me as much as it was by the movement itself. And more and more I thought that, at the very least, I would be an intermediary between the turmoil of the moment and times to come which would be more predictable and easier to understand.

I continued laboriously to transcribe in my notebooks tales I imagined that seemed more real to me than the actual history I was living.

And I kept many of these accounts even though I think they are indecipherable for the simple reason that they represent the period in its crude, unfinished form, before being sharpened up by the chlorine and acid treatment.

Writing was like being in a hidden sanctuary, a refuge from the day-to-day time of job and home.

Did you ever write?

It was about the only thing I did that allowed me to sit in sad cafés hour after hour, ritually ordering espressos, mixing in the sugar, and drinking them slowly, first warm, then cold, all the time being a source of intrigue for the regulars, who liked to watch me move with my set order from one notebook to the next. This behavior always set me apart in their eyes from the prostitutes or women stood up by their lovers. Writing wasn't a

MY STORY, YOUR STORY

way of just filling up time. On the contrary, it worked against time, struggling with it for space on the marble table tops, the square ones, round ones, speckled with sugar grains.

It was also a way of being different from others, without anyone really having to know what the difference was, since the only people who knew me at all were those who watched me in the cafés. But they didn't know where I lived or what my name was. It was a way of staying alive, at least in the eyes of others.

I put on hold the question of usefulness in writing and the issue of the social function of art, and also I put in parentheses notions of social class, the People, the Revolution.

I let myself slip into a kind of steady fever that numbed my senses—the way one feels during the first stages of drunkenness—but I was clear on the fact that I was living in the middle of a dictatorship and that I belonged to a class of people that suffered very little. I was an intellectual and my place was the city.

The only advantage of having what I wrote published seemed to be the uniformity that print would give to my handwriting, something which would also take some of the fever out of my writing and help with the anxiety I felt when I went through a day without getting anything down on paper.

But I never published anything at all because it was so difficult and because I thought that no one would read it, despite some friends having seen some pages of mine and insisting on arranging a publisher for me. They recognized themselves in what I wrote like in those mirrors in the amusement parks—there they were in the background, somewhat distorted but nevertheless they were there.

The print would help disguise the passion but like a magnifying glass with powers of a crystal ball, it would smooth out to oblivion the tremors and vibrations of my words, leaving the reader with nothing, or almost nothing; squashing the words flat, leaving them to rot like those apples that destroy people in Kafka's stories.

Once in print, all a book would show was the reflex and mechanical side of my writing but it would never get to what was underneath, to where the struggle was going on.

It was just a matter of observing things and transcribing the country exactly as it was: pretty foul, to be sure, but not so bad as some would have it.

EDUARDA DIONÍSIO

We never forgot the physical reality, the beaches and sand bars, the mountains, the forests we explored inch by inch; the regional differences in people, the open markets and fairs, the handwork, the striped blankets, the pine furniture, the earthenware and tin work, the rag rugs, the kerosene lamps, the gold trinkets on black velvet. We brought all these objects home like relics from the Real Portugal, the Portugal that was being buried by the government media, by the reactionary Church, by the programmed obscurantism. The relics of a lost people soon to be replaced by plastic saints.

We never knew whether we should worship or condemn the offerings we saw hanging by the thousands in churches everywhere, and in all the pilgrimages we made throughout Our Land, we never seemed to be able to talk with the people we came across, especially in the winter. The squares, the shops, and the cafés were always deserted.

And there was a heavy silence about the battles and the strikes that had been going on in some of these places.

It seemed like it might be possible to say something new by putting words in the order you wanted, either new words that suddenly came up or others finely tooled as from a machine shop, and at the same time, to combat the enemy with this work and defend the interests of those working from sunrise to sunset or under the infernal light of offices and factories, still abused and unfree. I still think that it would have been possible, that it had been possible. But at the same time, it was so difficult and many of the people who could have done it didn't have time or were afraid because things might not turn out the way they wanted or they would lose their social standing and their power. Solidarity was possible but there was a high price on it.

I think there were those who tried but few could endure the test which was really hard, especially since the struggle was on two fronts: the awesome challenge of creating through words places and people that had never existed before and that of the day-to-day talking to people in the movement, convincing them that they were right, and reminding them that there was no reason to compromise on solidarity.

The last years of the dictatorship perhaps weren't so brutally violent as the first stage and did you notice, then, how the desire

MY STORY, YOUR STORY

to own things—household items and such—became almost insane? Cars, always shined up, carpets on all the floors, curtains, all sorts of objects arranged so that they could easily be seen, usually things made out of plastic, gadgets and tools for all occasions, bought up the minute they appeared on the market; and later there were the plants, the pet birds, the fish, and on those camping trips, when people normally relax a little, everything was still in its prescribed place: little contraptions for hanging utensils, towels, stoves, everything just so, seemingly unused, smooth and clean looking, maintaining the appearance of invulnerability. And there was a growing impatience towards those who were close—husbands, wives, children—and at the same time, the fear and confusion about an unknown dictator increased, along with the fear of unbelievable torture that could happen to anyone at any time, fear that the dictator was listening, fear of his iron grip, those bony, hairy claws snatching up gestures and conversations, censuring all dreaming and desire, shoving us all back into our houses where it seemed to be safe—so long as we never violated the no-thinking laws, the know-nothing law, the laws against creativity and imagination, against wanting things to be different. Just so long as we did what everyone else was doing and never took a real deep breath, nor tuned our radios to the world, nor warned others of the risk they were running.

Mistrust grew thick and permanent like a cloud not breaking up after the rain, mistrust of those who were around at odd hours in the morning or at nightfall, of those that lingered for hours in the cafés with their newspapers open, of new friends, of people at work who were either too nice or not nice at all.

There was a mistrust of everything that wasn't absolutely normal—of idle time, of people who were alone, of sensational accounts.

Whenever we responded, it was indirectly. Silence and a sense of void took roots in people, establishing their own rigorous and tragic pattern.

Less and less we registered outrage at repugnant events we heard about, the assassinations those in power were committing —whether back in the woods or out in the open, in public squares of big cities—the behind-the-back set-ups, the betrayals, the kangaroo courts, the books dismembered by the stubby blue

EDUARDA DIONÍSIO

pencils of the censors, the constant lying which had become a patriotic virtue, the helpless situation of the prisoners, the courtrooms stacked with assassins and torturers drowning out the voices of others, witnesses courageously saying what they thought but knowing that, at that particular moment, nothing would mean anything since the police had already decided, often with a little help from the dictator himself.

The capacity for indignation diminished after hearing accounts of violence and terror. The spirit of compliance spread wide, settling into the silence of everyday life almost imperceptibly. We became further and further removed from History.

At the same time, there were more and more divisions between factions, more betrayals of loyalties which were excused because hopes for some kind of victory seemed to have fallen apart; also, a greater sense of our own weakness and all the while, a harder line in the way we carried out political activity. Certainty about anything seemed to dissolve almost invisibly along with the magical power that had before kept us alive, and we felt as if we had been taken to that inescapable point where death was imminent.

It was a final phase or almost that.

There was a certain air about us that signalled the downfall—the moral downfall—of the empire. Cases of dissolution multiplied: of the qualities some of us had had before; of the families some of us had formed with determination; and of the bold love relationships we had undertaken.

We were the vanguard of that downfall, indulging ourselves with homosexuals the way we did with the aging clowns at the beach circuses we used to go to, calling up the romantic spirit we saved for such occasions.

It was then that we began to go around championing the lives of marginals and we liked walking in Mayer Park, not out of habit like everyone else, but admiring from a distance the whores and the go-go girls as if they were art objects in a museum or social anomalies. Their beauty was almost literary for us, above all when they looked out from behind their mascara; or at night, in the clubs, when we watched them kicking their legs up, working with a touch of fever—symptom of a sickness the doctors couldn't detect—a low-grade infection that would pass.

The semi-suicides had begun: escapes from the city, hiding out in someone's house where you acted like you were born again once they found you.

The interactions with one another started out there too, while walking along the water until early morning, and then these intense contacts dissolving the next day back in Lisbon, right in the middle of some park or café.

None of this was ever confused with a mere coming to one's senses or with some kind of discovery that you make as an adolescent. This was nothing less than the prelude to the Desert Age brought on by the erosion of Western Civilization.

We were incapable of living or sharing any kind of joy together, probably because we were all wrapped up in ourselves and in making a living, however sporadically: there were the translations, the surveys, public opinion studies, the jobs living off the rich families, the same ones that supported us endlessly like overgrown children.

A certain paranoia spread among us.

In this rather lugubrious fare we responded to others' censure of us by cultivating disdain for them.

* * *

I don't know if you stayed home on the days of the twenty-fifth and twenty-sixth of April, if you too were already thinking at that time that history was something that was made by others; I don't know if you would have been with me in front of the prison where they were still holding people. It was a strange kind of vigil to have after the miracle. On the one hand, it was more like the early ones during the resistance with people from then relearning the old songs, adding their support; on the other, although we wanted to think the repression was over, it seemed to keep on coming, but we didn't know from where.

For the first time, the cries of protest were something other than symbolic and those movement people, activated just by being there, were demanding the release of other comrades, some of whom had little use for each other.

EDUARDA DIONÍSIO

People had just come alive, scarcely knowing to whom their demands were directed, but they had the enthusiasm that comes with the first victory over fear and danger. The prison opened its doors and friends and comrades went out into the middle of the night, which had already turned cold. Everyone was crying—probably for very different reasons.

So many people—where did they all come from? Were there really that many people in the city? I had met you a couple of days before, so it was in April, and I think I saw you leaning up against a lamppost, looking at the crowds, at the banners, up in the sky. Or maybe it wasn't you, but someone about your height and with that look you have. Looking at the crowd made a strong impression: never had there been so many in one place at one time; all of a sudden, people were learning new words and new songs and there was a new confidence, open and strong; even the old enemies, the generals, were glorified; and the old guard, with its funereal pomp, was advancing against the demonstrations of laughter and irreverence.

Apotheosis. Many people were crying and from their refuges, animals, human as well as others, listened and watched the open zone. The leaders and heroes appeared at the rostrum, some of them thinking that all those people out there, or at least most of them, were their possession. There were those who were hoarse from so much shouting and who didn't know that the calls for order were coming from other countries and that they might spell death.

I think that some—I don't know if you were one of them—began to walk with a different step, without any concern for time, hour after hour, through city streets, down by the docks, and from one house to another.

They began to dress differently, as if they were perpetually on days off, and never again did office buildings and schools have that somber, cold look.

Freedom became part of everyday life and leaders and authorities of all kinds stopped being afraid of blue jeans, which almost everyone was wearing, and of the absence of ties, and of long hair on men.

The new country breathed freely in all sorts of ways but at the

MY STORY, YOUR STORY

same time there was the nagging feeling that this moment was merely historic and that it could never be repeated with the same intensity—getting rid of hats, ties, three-piece suits, being accepted, putting up their own posters of Che, Marx, and Lenin on the walls of the state offices where they worked.

Streets and houses belonged to the people that lived in them. They no longer had to be bought or rented. We helped ourselves to everything—schools, public squares, monuments, walls, public transportation—and we demonstrated that it was all ours in conversations with others who were searching around for what was left of the oppressors in the old spaces that they used to occupy.

We all did a great deal of talking because it was now our city, we hated the dictatorship and we had destroyed the terror inflicted by some on others and the terror within ourselves.

Life was lived ardently day and night and the clocks began to tell time differently now. The old rhythms came undone so that after a few days you didn't even know how you had ever lived before. You had the power of feeling that every word and gesture was your own. Things happening weren't just on the radio and in the newspapers because we ourselves had been there. The dimensions of the city became smaller and smaller and we dashed from one end of it to another, adding our support to the momentum of History. We no longer lived at home. We lived out there in the city, in the squares, on the streets.

People sprang up everywhere like plants in the clear space of April and May days, and in varying degrees, they all shared the common feeling of victory—whether they came by air or by boat, no matter how they had lived out the years of the dictatorship; others emerged cautiously from prison darkness or from their lives of submission, obscurity, and domestic routine, suddenly transformed from dutiful heads of silent households into dashing leaders with projects for a new tomorrow; they claimed their place in the struggle, in the liberated zones, filling up the new, open spaces with themselves.

Others came who had long been used to endless political meetings during the resistance period, with their rules and dim lights, the intricate game of give-and-take, trade-offs, slow gains, conversations where certain things had been taboo, where silences had been alive with meaning, and where the stakes had been as intense and calculated as the shrewd livestock trading that went on during those somber village fair days. These people emerged armed with their experience and tried to dominate the newcomers who at times looked disoriented and made rash moves.

Those that refused to stick to the old political agenda worked out in manuals and pamphlets during the resistance and who didn't want to associate with the petrified leadership, learned quickly in the course of those days all about class questions, about who really was on which side, about forms of organization to which they had been oblivious. And they saw themselves beginning to move as fast as the events around them. They saw themselves written up in the newspapers and they were on radio newscasts all over the country.

Some stopped from time to time to ask themselves about what others might be thinking about all the sudden changes, about the guns and the carnation revolution. The old people off in the villages with their cottages, bean crops, and nettles; the concierge lady whom they suspected of being a stoolpigeon for the dictatorship; or the fisherman they had met looking for eels in the lagoons when they were on vacation.

But there never was time to stop and find out because the revolution just kept gaining momentum.

translated by Charles Cutler

SHIMMERING UMBRELLAS

(excerpt)

by

Teolinda Gersão

TEOLINDA GERSÃO

Teolinda Gersão is a member of the youngest generation of women who began to publish in the 1980s and, like many of her generation in and outside of Portugal, she is the modern superwoman. In her case, she is wife and mother, novelist and academic. Born in the university city of Coimbra, Teolinda Gersão earned a Ph.D. in German literature and, after spending some time as a lecturer in Portuguese at the University of Berlin, joined the faculty of the University of Lisbon, where she teaches and produces scholarly work in her chosen field.

Gersão's first two novels, O Silêncio *(*Silence, *1981) and* Paisagem com Mulher e Mar ao Fundo *(*Landscape with Woman and Sea in the Background, *1982) are sensitive and lyrical explorations of women's entrapment, particularly in the troubled era of Salazar, who appears in the second novel as the everpresent and threatening figure known only by the initials O.S. Gender issues and political oppression are the dual matrices for the thematics of the novels.*

Gersão's third piece of fiction, Os Guarda-chuvas Cintilantes *(*Shimmering Umbrellas, *1984) is a work of another stripe. Cast in the form of a writer's journal, it brings together in a seemingly arbitrary fashion not only the writer's fictions but her explorations of the self (sometimes an "I", at other times a "she"); glimpses of day-to-day existence, with children who bear the names of animals and a dog with quasi-human capacities; and always the volatile and elusive umbrellas. A diary, the narrative nevertheless challenges the notion of "diary": directly, in a metafictional mode; more subtly, in its shattering of the sequentiality normally identified with that genre's essence. The result is an apparent chaos that awaits the collaboration of the reader to give it unity and closure—as does any other diary, the author suggests. The translation gives an accurate sense of the aesthetic whole; it begins with the opening pages of the novel, skips to other passages representative of the novel's thematic variety, and ends with the penultimate section of Gersão's book.*

Works by Teolinda Gersão

Silêncio, *1981*
Paisagem com Mulher e Mar ao Fundo, *1982*
Os Guarda-Chuvas Cintilantes, *1984*
O Cavalo de Sol, *1989*

SHIMMERING UMBRELLAS

Sunday, the first

The small dome of days. Round, curved, transparent. Behind, the large empty sky, a fictitious sky that at times seemed tinted ashen blue or black, depending on the changes in the wind and the unfathomable configuration of things.

The distinctly different seasons of that region, the year's wheel spinning on its head, the leaves, the birds, the trees, the sky, the colors, the rain . . .

The umbrellas, she remembered. In a dream she stole umbrellas: one of them was propped in the middle of the street between painted boards of red and white stripes, indicating construction, illuminated by small tin lamps, and she stole it, soaking her feet

---

From *Os Guarda-chuvas Cintilantes* (*Shimmering Umbrellas*), by Teolinda Gersão (Lisbon: O Jornal, 1984).

SHIMMERING UMBRELLAS

in the puddles and letting herself be splashed with the mud of the quickly passing cars on the asphalt which rapidly veered to the right at the last moment so as not to run her over. She was risking her life she realized, to stretch her hand forth so incautiously, but at the very moment she was about to grab it, a car hit them all, throwing them up in the air, in confused pieces, and now she walked along the street, chasing after another umbrella, indifferent as one who thinks of something else while all the time ready to jab at one as soon as it became distracted—but it too was aware of her, it noted her, as it swung prudently from one side to the other, looking furtively behind—and now it has suddenly escaped through the doorway, and she not even able to touch it, although she rushed to stick her fingers out . . .

And now it is another one lying gently at her feet. Slowly twirling on itself, as if she had provoked it with a quick whistle, almost inaudible, a puff, a tiny animal sound like a soft beating of wings.

She went on a bit, pretending not to see it (a silk one, of glass, of tin foil, illuminating itself like a dome, a glass window, depending upon how the sun hits it or the wind strikes it), I am in the doorway between two glass windows with mirrors, I put my hands in the pockets of my overcoat and pretend not to see (a cat catching a bird, I think, a cat closing its eyes so as to become invisible, sensing that the bird will not see it if it creeps up, one foot after the other, without opening its eyes, with velvet gestures, faking the motion, the body taut, mechanical, without any thoughts, just a bundle of reflexes as if moved by an inner spring).

It slides along until it nearly reaches my side, it then recedes a bit and curls up into a ball—a walking turtle, a winged turtle that would take off if I came any closer—I catch it suddenly and it comes undone, rests in my hand like some dark unformed substance, a mountain of tainted leaves.

Saturday, the third

The first rain. Peaceful, light, killing any trace of faint nostalgia

TEOLINDA GERSÃO

inside. To lift her head, like a tree lifting its leaves. The hoped-for rain of the summer ahead, secretly awaited within herself. To see the windows quake in the summer wind, to secure ever more tightly the wooden doorways, latching the bolt above, to see at a glance the small village square, flooded by sunlight, vacant in the afternoon heat, and to know the rain would return, to desire it fervently as if it would diminish the body's tension —a light rain in which all her limbs would stretch out, alive, awake, but so very gentle and relaxed as if they had been sleeping, all would suddenly become so close as if it were the rain that brought us all things and left them shining, soaking wet, glistening within reach, with contact restored, the profound harmony between herself and the world—a difficult, unstable harmony because she insisted upon always living rigorously, with an unswerving attention even when she slept—the rigor, for example, with which she controlled or demolished dreams, forcing herself to remember them, forcing them to jump through flaming hoops the imagined flowers finally forming a bouquet, the flowers of the shade, of sun, of sand, to control the wind, to learn to ride the wind, to draw a blue line around the sea the hard acrobatics of her body, at the same time wild and geometric, the difficult inner exercises, the mortal leaps with blindfolded eyes, upon a strand of barbed wire stretched out between the possible and the impossible.

Monday, the fourteenth

That whole year lasted one 'single day and then flew off more quickly than a bird through the half-opened window.

(Later she would often scold herself for having left the window half open.)

Thursday, the eighth

They would suddenly open as if they had exploded, she would become somewhat frightened as if a gun had just gone off in her hand, others were broken and would not open, nor was there any chance they eventually would, there were also striking, foldable days that would keep growing in size and, when care-

SHIMMERING UMBRELLAS

fully folded up, could be saved inside the pocketbook like a fan or a handkerchief, they said, but it was not true, she at least was never to use them a second time, she had already thought about ways to better use them but none of them ever proved to be practicable, it was necessary to live thus, throwing them away or putting them aside and not using them again, it was a shame, she thought, turning the dying umbrella around in her hands, it was a shame, she said, because it was beautiful, it had been beautiful, with brown circles recalling leaves that matched that clear October weather, but it was always like that, they quickly lost their color and became transparent, the spines would bend, the silk would wrinkle and tear, it would lose its shape and remain there in her hands like some inconsistent viscous mass, she would like to photograph the unusually beautiful ones, save their light, the memory of their light, but in the photographs they always seemed so different, nothing was more untrue than photographs, sometimes she tried to transfer the light from one to another and they seemed to come alive again, under this borrowed light, sometimes they seemed more beautiful than ever as if the true light were this one in which she projected them—discovering in them colors she had not seen at the time, designs that only now were revealed and had previously been invisible, or else she had not known how to look—but she could not use them again and knowing this now did not change anything.

It was untrue that they should last, she said, they went out like lamps, only once, one single time, each one would burn once then explode, implode, collapse on itself, trails of tattered silk on the floor, scattered about a crushed handle—

At other times a line of black umbrellas ran behind her, chasing her or forming a peripatetic wall before her that she never succeeded in getting beyond—but it was untrue as well, because the walls were unmoving and it was she who was running behind, and it was her fault when she only chose black umbrellas, she could not complain, she even knew why, secretly, she found them fascinating, phosphorescent like the wings of a raven, slightly (or deeply) terrifying. But fear excited her as well, exalted her . . .

TEOLINDA GERSÃO

Monday, the twelfth

It is not a diary, the critic said, because it is not a record of what happened each day. Lacking, therefore, the distinctive characteristic of this genre or sub-genre in which a work tries to situate itself, the work referred to is from the outset excluded from the specific form to which it claims adherence. Dixi.

. . . .

Thursday, the seventh

The small daily writing, to leave a mark in time, a trace in the sands, to prove that I am alive—Monday, Tuesday, Thursday, two, five, seven, twenty-four, this painstaking responsibility, or escape, this static accounting, passive, applied, methodic, monotonous, academic—oh, lord, I wasn't cut out for this, I've always been so mistaken in my calculations in life—but where does this intimate belief in ascertaining the problem, in spite of everything, come from?

Sunday, the eleventh

I have become exhausted from trying to grasp the world, the author said.

I don't even have time to make a telephone call. I run to one end trying to grasp cities, to another end to get at rivers, to yet another to seize bridges. If I close my eyes for one single minute, the universe begins to waver and falls. Because it is out of myself that time and space originate.

Tuesday, the fifteenth

That which I look at exists, that which I ignore remains forever in non-being—diaries are profoundly ridiculous, Pip says, the philosophy professor who would secretly like to be a poet. The world does not rotate around the author, it is completely indifferent to the author, the world doesn't give a damn about Barthes's not liking Chinese evergreen trees, it doesn't give a damn, give a damn, give a damn—diaries and the like are the most ridiculous of all literary forms.

SHIMMERING UMBRELLAS

Friday, the seventeenth

Slowly the body enters the day. Detaching itself from the spongy mass of sleep and cutting out new surfaces for itself, sensitive like pointed edges. Outside, above the garden, the early morning. To listen to the birds, the branches beating against the glass windows. The noise of the airplanes passing. Seen from the plane, the city was a vast cemetery with millions of stones, tombs that closer up, as the plane swerved and the wings lowered, became skyscrapers, chaotic and white.

She could have enjoyed Brazil, just as she had enjoyed Africa. With the body, the tongue, the skin, her sex. Just as she enjoyed the forest, in spite of its heat, lack of water, dust, hardships, thirst, fatigue. To forget all that for the pleasure of the earth, the landscape, the silence, the wild smells in the air. To rediscover her animal skin, to live content as body movement, as breathing.

But that city was of stone, she thought, as she went into the kitchen. And there was little in it to love.

Wednesday, the fifth

I am absolutely gorgeous, the author said, fascinated. Absolutely gorgeous, absolutely gorgeous, absolutely gorgeous. So much so that I cannot tear my eyes from the mirror. And all that exists I am tempted to convert into "I". Because I only have eyes for myself.

She sat down in the chair, crossed her legs, and began to devour the world. She swallowed and swallowed, becoming enormously fat, and the swelling of the I was so great that, at a certain moment, it burst and broke into a shower of scattered pieces.

And then, patiently, on all fours, she looked for the pieces here and there and began to glue them back together with Super Glue.

TEOLINDA GERSÃO

Thursday, the twentieth

Diaries are perverse, Pip says. The author is a fragmented being to whom the reader's eye lends an illusory unity—the author's need of the reader to exist, to exist loosely, potentially, in a quick show of three minutes under a spotlight, before a peephole where the reader/voyeur peeks in, after having inserted a coin in the slot of the box—diaries are the most idiotic of forms and the most perverse of all literature.

. . . .

Wednesday, the twentieth

And since she liked to bamboozle them and laugh at them at certain moments, in order to knock them completely off guard, she told them the story of the man who talked:

There once was a man who never stopped talking, he talked all the time, as if he had a spring loose (she continued). At the door of a friend who wasn't at home he remained four hours talking with the wife, it was a cold and rainy day and each time she asked him to come in he politely refused, because he thought it inappropriate to enter with the husband gone, even though the rest of the family was at home, so he bid them farewell, shook hands each time that she, frozen, insisted upon his coming inside, but after bidding them farewell he did not go away and continued talking until the wife, exhausted, resigned, and in turn equally over-polite, asked that two chairs be brought, and they remained or he remained, the rest of the afternoon talking, she seated inside and he outside in the rain, then the husband arrived through the gate to the yard and, informed of the situation by the family, did not invite him inside, he bid him farewell with a slap on the back and began to shut the door, but the man was quicker and shoved his foot in the doorway and continued talking, now more furiously, with more urgency, speeding up the rhythm of his sentences, even running the risk of crushing his foot, until the friend let up on the doorknob somewhat and he pulled his foot away, giving a sigh of relief and taking this opportunity to barrage them one more time with a spate of words,

SHIMMERING UMBRELLAS

this time through the very narrow crack in the closing door where he almost caught his mouth because talking was his lot, his way of existing. Another time he entered into the house of another friend with the wife and the nine or perhaps twelve children, he was passing through the neighborhood by accident and he decided to pay him a visit, he said, when he travelled by taxi between two train stations, he stayed for lunch and dinner and, as he didn't stop talking, they all wound up sleeping there, in improvised beds, the nine children or twelve children and the wife, all but the man who kept on talking, and for two days he talked without stopping, missing all the trains until the friend arrived in desperation, grabbed them all, put them in a taxi, took them to the station, and threw them onto the train, the last to get on was the man who talked, with his foot half on the train he turned around one more time to finish his sentence at the very moment that the train began to move, but with the jolt he lost his balance, fell off the train, and continued talking, at the station, waving his arms at the same time both to his friend, who turned his back on him, frightened, and fled, and to the family who, perplexed, were still on the train.

. . . .

Thursday, the nineteenth

"I," she said, when they lost patience listening to the story and went away, and she returned calmly to the heart of the problem, recapitulating the givens. I, she said, and the word was a plum pit in the mouth, rolling over the tongue, but outside on the surface, I, she repeated, and looked up at the sky as if it were an echo, I the intersecting point of people, lives, times, spaces, dimensions, the intersecting point of planes, lights, colors, various sounds.

Diaries remained equivocal as to whether the I, the real, and time existed, were definable and fixed—but the truth was not like that, as anyone with a sufficiently corrosive eye to see it would know, she suspected.

I, she tried once again, but it was always an inconsistent truth, I leaf, wind, sand, foam—I stone, sea, insect, sleeping animal, or animal awake and expectant, ears raised and all the senses alert, ready to pounce to another side, a non-existent side.

. . . .

Friday, the eighteenth

Not the fixed and conventional image of the mirror but an image in flight. But who had the strength to break the law of the mirror?

Her face floating in the waters, always reflecting itself anew and going off, dissolving water flowing, becoming cloudy, roiled, at the least gust of wind—

The page like a mirror, reflex, separation and obstacle between a subject and its object—she tried to traverse it, in writing, to penetrate it with the fine point of the pen and hold on to her face at the other side, but the pen only slid about, without harming the paper, it spun around, danced on the surface, it could keep on spinning endlessly, it would never cross the paper, it would always remain on the other side.

Distance alone between the I and its double was measured in writing, the fleeting shadow which always eluded her anew.

Alienation was writing's real name, she discovered.

. . . .

Sunday, the twenty-third

Sometimes I imagine a totally repressed world, Pip says, taking off his sandals and putting his feet on the edge of the table, persecuted by televisions they are forced to watch, with programs they are compelled to look at, while other machines control them, spy on them, television circuits that follow them everywhere, even to the bathroom or to bed, watching them all the time, even when they urinate, defecate, make love, or sleep, even inside their sleep because they have to sleep with electronic

SHIMMERING UMBRELLAS

contraptions hooked to their heads and connected to a gigantic computer whose terminal is in the control of the State where dreams are projected on a screen and analyzed by a special committee, named exclusively for that purpose, those who have subversive dreams will be set apart from the community and made to pay a penalty, that is why there are so many sedatives for sale made to facilitate a tranquil sleep without dreams.

Such a world is close at hand, we are only a hair's breadth from it and it will not be long until we are there, we live in an unreal square, with eyes riveted on the transitory real square, we only feel secure when surrounded by images, suspended from images, when they no longer appear we do not know who we are, because outside of these images we have no identity. "Who am I?" I ask myself in the mirror and the answer "Pip" is without any context, because the image of the mirror is fixed, not fluid, and for this reason it forces me to stop, but this halting frightens me, I only know how to live moving forward, in the illusion of the images' movements, "who am I?" I ask again and nobody answers, the house is deserted, the world is deserted, only when the images begin again do I feel calm once more, oblivious to myself, imitating the images, copying them all through the day, living effortlessly because they furnish me with an already made model for everything—opening, as the image demonstrates, a can of soup, pea purée, the new and tested defroster, leafing through a recent issue of a newly published newspaper, trying out the new granulated instant coffee, the best tasting according to the image, and I taste it, now comes the cigarette, golden tobacco, from Virginia, the man in the image says, lighting one up, blowing a blue puff of smoke into the air and inhaling its smell: "even its smell is glowing and golden," he says turning towards me, and I try one out, lighting one just like his, sitting back more comfortably on the sofa, dipping into forgetfulness, letting my time, free memory and free association of ideas and things come undone, because the images leave me no space to invent anything, they will prevent me from thinking, from feeling, an anaesthesia, a hypnosis, I sit down on the sofa and the world disappears, it will come back after I have had my dinner on a tray and cut my meat without looking at it, in order not to take my eyes away from the images, even the sound of the knitting needles bothers me, the opening of a door, the turning of the pages of a book, Giza's nail file smoothing her nails, I want a space where everything disappears, like a sleep, to fill my head with its images, as if it were sand—shut up, I will holler at the children, because no one but the images has permission to talk and they cannot be interrupted, to educate children is to teach them to watch television, I think confusedly, tilting my head backwards, to keep them wide-eyed in front of the screen, even when they seem distracted something sticks, it is engraved in their memory, that is why the obligatory number of hours for watching television will wind up being legislated, inversely proportionate to the age of the subject, the younger the individual, the more apt to assimilate and therefore a longer obligatory time, only for the senior citizens, when there is virtually no more receptive capacity, the time of watching television may be substantially reduced, limited to just a few hours a day, each one choosing his or her own hours, since it is no longer mandatory to live in such promiscuity with the images.

"This is the so-called new contemplation," I hear the voice of the invited professor saying in the middle of the screen. With his hands crossed on top of the polished table, with its vase of flowers and glass of water. "In such a way, technology allows us to recuperate those values of the past which would otherwise be lost forever.

"The first stage of contemplation is indifference in relation to the surrounding universe that becomes colorless and remote, increasingly evaporating until it disappears completely. It is at this point that the second and third stages of contemplation take place, respectively.

"With the fourth stage of contemplation one becomes more and more external until the relationship to the body is completely lost—to the body of others, but above all to one's own. This occurs to such an extent that if someone touches him or, in some cases, if someone pricks him with a pin, the person will have no sensation of it. He will become weightless.

"At the fifth and last stage the fusion with the image is total. One goes inside the screen, trespassing the barriers and finally

SHIMMERING UMBRELLAS

entering into another universe, into the longed-for dimension—"

Then I become terrified and begin to fight back, forcing myself to slow down, Pip says, but astonished I realize that I do not know where I left myself, where my body is, why the images fill all things, take up my space, push me out, make me lose my balance, suddenly I no longer know what my life is and what it is not, what belongs to me and what does not, they are overwhelming images, omnipresent, galloping, falling in a powerful rush towards the inside of the hours, dissolving, destroying time, I turn my head so as not to see them but there are images on the other wall as well, a voice and video are there on all sides as if the walls were a mirror,

then I become desperate and begin to move towards them, a hammer in hand, but when I am about to lower it in one fell swoop and break the machine, the images quickly break up the room which, in a fraction of a second, becomes a tiny rectangle of light, retreating inside of nothingness, disappearing in the night with us inside.

. . . .

Thursday, the second

People think of literature as an additional realm of experience, Pip says, but they forget that it is merely potential experience which cannot be used in any effective manner. An author invents characters who struggle with precisely that which he avoids, he remains calmly seated while they fight it out, for his part, something of him is exposed while something else remains safely at home, behind the curtains, where his feet are nicely toasted before the hearth. And the reader, the potential author, repeats the same experience, doubly frustrating because he does not even bother himself to do the writing, a much smaller chore suffices, that of following, of gliding along, slowed down, line after line, behind his eyes, and the energy expended in getting through the book is no longer fruitfully expended energy when going through life, and what is worse, an exalted feeling of having gone through it is created, but it is completely illusory.

TEOLINDA GERSÃO

—But, deep down, you would sell your soul to the devil to be able to write a book, I scream, because today he has finally brought me to my boiling point.

—That's right, I am the one who should write books, he says, without changing, I have all one needs to write them, a keen eye, a way with words, I say so many things, in fact, that are really pages of a book and, if you are not a complete ass, you would use them in your next novel, I can see perfectly well in your eyes when what I say interests you, click, there it is, an instant, an idea, a captured thing, you go on living at my expense because you do not invent anything, you only record, but I invent, I am a writer, only I am a writer without any work because all works imply contradictions, to write one it would first be necessary to know what literature is and what value it has, but literature does not justify itself and that is why I will never write, because what has no justification is not worth being made, but I am nevertheless a writer. Even though I can never write I am no less a writer—the true writer is precisely one who is conscious of the impossibility of writing,

—And those who write books are what, I ask, furious.

—They are scribes, he says. With a certain embarrassment, they pass over all the difficulties out of a total incapacity to see them. That's what you do.

. . . .

Monday, the twenty-third

—He is neither a loner nor a vagabond by nature, Lu says as he strokes Dax. A dog is sociable, a member of the household, of the family, it has the clan instinct and a deep sense of human relations. A dog is human.

Pure relationships where intelligence, beauty, culture, social status do not have the slightest importance. Absolute relationships like those we only see in childhood, I think. Lu could be a tramp, and he would follow him happily to the end of the world. In the whole world, he alone would be his dog, and only he would be his master, thought the dog.

SHIMMERING UMBRELLAS

The two setting out from the garden gate. Dax running ahead, discovering, looking around, sniffing, the world revealing itself new and different each morning before its eyes, its ears, its delicate dog snout, coming back again from behind, wagging its tail and calling the man, showing him once again the things he had shown him before but that he had forgotten, with his weak eyes, weak ears, weak nose all human, passing by things without seeing them. To discover the world, why was the human body so insufficient, so incapable, too tall, removed from the ground, going through things as if things were only an idea. To really know, it was necessary to have a dog's heart, the young body of a dog, swift and open in the clear morning, passing through the world with all its senses awakened, attentive to all signs, entirely free and without memory, fixed on the instant.

He knows, Dax. He has discovered as well that the world changes in accordance with the company one keeps. With Lu, the world is that sense of discovery in the sun-drenched morning. An alertness, expectant and controlled. It's not the same as with children. Rolling in the grass, jumping all over their skirts with his dirty paws, always in movement with a crazy kind of joy that prevents him from being totally attentive to anything, running in all directions at the same time, with three leaps he is at the foot of the low wooden gate and with just one more jump he is once again at the foot of the wall, running to the other side, one never knows which side he is running towards because Dax is pure movement, ears, paws, tail, hair quivering in the air, and his heart, when they catch him, silky and alive, a furry brown heart framed by the sunlight, a heart of ambling grass, running through the grasses, pressing their faces with his hot ears, interested in all things and vibrating, learning so well all about the world on his own, even when he does not understand and gets everything mixed up. He has such an original way of laughing and becoming scared, of showing astonishment at things, he gives himself over totally to sensations, because all of them seem good to him, the smells especially, he can make out at a distance the thousand different smells in the air, he chooses one or two and takes off running, because it is not so much the form or color of the world but its smell that interests him. In short, he has learned to recognize even the most difficult smells, the smell of stones, of water, of invisible ants, underground, the inconsistent smell of rain beginning, which then becomes the dizzying, overwhelming smell of wet earth—nothing holds, in fact, as many smells as the earth, they vary with the temperature, the humidity, the time of day, but the sun equally possesses a thousand different smells, depending upon what it blends with, there is the best smell of all, that of the sun mixing with the earth, but there is also the smell of its fusion with plants, with lime, with stone, with wood, with brick, with urine, with manure, or simply with the particles of dust, the thousand haphazard particles that we see hanging in the streams of light, in the great crisscrossing streams—oh, if they were to enter the realm of the visible—all things forever in balance, taking off at full speed, going forward and backward, the dog romping about in the grass, his barks mixing with the light, the clear day, the tree branches shaking, because there is a great tree as well, at the foot of the yard, open to all the birds but without catching any of them in its great transparent green hands, where the sun trickles down, its feet below the earth soaking in some obscure river, the tree running in the garden with the children on its shoulders, sometimes singing, sometimes yelling, at night, when the wind blows, with him jumping around, halting all of a sudden, taking off again with the tail raised high.

. . . .

Thursday, the twenty-ninth

Stories like waves, coming and going, disintegrating, reorganizing themselves, beginning again, continuing, always continuing. One forgets them and they return, or perhaps they were other stories, different, similar. Or all of them were perhaps the same pounding wave, infinitely repetitious and doubled over.

Listening to stories, each time hoping they turn into something else, that they will at some point make the qualitative leap and become transformed—perhaps into real life? But life was not a superior kind in this chain.

SHIMMERING UMBRELLAS

Saturday, the twelfth

The piece of paper like a trap into which life falls, unwarned, unheeding, stumbling as it passes through my clever hand which stealthily rises, becoming an obstruction to its movement forward,

Monday, the sixteenth

Words like nets in which she tried to catch the universe—the tiny mesh of the net which she tried so hard to connect, but there was always a point in which the net would break and the universe would spill out,

the difficulty in connecting things, the foot with the grass, the roof with the wall, the sun with the house, the bus with the tree, the machine with the shadow, the man with the dog, what was the relationship between the things she saw and were they all part of some whole? Nothing was a whole, it was she who tired herself out running behind things, trying to connect things together with threads, giving them meaning they didn't have before—and that they let fall again, refusing it always.

We have however the wind, the winter, the tree, the wall, she said. We have however the sun, the open window, the open house, intact and uninhabited—the people have gone away taking their suitcases and coats, their shoes and books, their brushes and problems, and she had not the slightest desire to follow them, to look at them, to understand them, she remained instead quiet thus one long minute among the objects which all of a sudden became fascinating and perfect, delivered unto themselves and without any links whatsoever to other things.

She could tell a thousand stories, invent a thousand stories she thought stretching out in the grass, but they were all untrue, no story at all really existed.

. . . .

TEOLINDA GERSÃO

Saturday, the twelfth

—Come, come, the umbrellas called, marching suddenly in the night, circling around themselves in unison like enormous sunflowers to music,

we whirl about with more or less rapidity depending upon how the wind, or hope, or happiness propels us with more or less force, when hope is high, or the love strong, we whirl about in space at a dizzying speed and we scintillate, we beckon forth from galaxy to galaxy, and our light leaves a message that can be picked up even millions of years after we have died out.

—come, come, we are about to leave, they whistled in a low voice in her ears, just a step and we will take you with us,

such a passageway opens only once in your life, they insisted as they stirred about, making a noise with their wings that sounded like the wind, only once does the moon intersect the sun at midnight and the trees sing and the clover quivers like a flock of birds in flight, only once does the lion wait at the door of its house, with a purple ring in its mouth and a diamond between its claws, and the virgin lights her candle while in the cradle the small twins lie fast asleep and the scales become quiet because all the winds have calmed down, while in the fish bowl the water finally ceases to flow and the fish are all scattered in the sky of glass, stirring up the dust there.

—No, no, she said, if I were to go with you I would have less a voice than I do down here.

—If you do not come you lose your chance, we do not know when we will come back, we will open up to others the way you now refuse—place one foot before you and come with us, why do you remain locked in your body, at the frontier, at the limit,

—No, she said, a voice at least would make a difference, therefore so long, have a good trip, she said waving her hand while the group of umbrellas took off and vanished.

translated by Susan M. Brown

THE DEVIL'S MOUNTAIN

(excerpt)

by

Hélia Correia

HÉLIA CORREIA

Hélia Correia is a member of the youngest generation of Portuguese women pursuing successful literary careers today. Born in the late 1940s in the monumental city of Mafra, she is a teacher of Portuguese and French in a secondary school in the Lisbon area. Hélia Correia began writing as a poet but soon turned to the fiction that has brought her recognition. Her first novel, O Separar das Aguas (The Parting of the Waters), *was published in 1981, and half a dozen more have followed since then.*

Hélia Correia's fiction is informed by a fascination with mystery in two different configurations: enigma and fantasy. It assimilates the popular superstition of her native region, the folk culture that is as much a part of rural Portuguese consciousness as it is of the world of the Latin American Gabriel García Márquez. García Márquez has indeed been a presence in Correia's literary consciousness as has Agustina Bessa-Luís, another appropriator and creator of rural myths. Like Bessa-Luís, Hélia Correia is a sibylline witness to telluric and otherwise subliminal forces. Her characters are modern urban men as well as rural folk of both sexes but all are governed by an incomprehensible, inescapable fate. Her women are especially endowed with demonic energies. Correia's highly idiosyncratic style, with its jarring associations, also appears to emerge directly from the unconscious of a bewitched spinner of tales and enhances the oniric quality of her short narratives.

Correia is fascinated by other traditional literary modes and genres as well. In A Senda Erótica (The Erotic Path), *for example, she intentionally resurrects that nineteenth-century synthesis of journalism and fiction, the serial novel. This murder mystery, published as a book in 1988, was originally written in weekly installments for the magazine section of the Lisbon newspaper,* O Jornal.

Montedemo *(*The Devil's Mountain, *1983), from which the following selection it taken, is one of Correia's most successful* works. *It is the story of a mountain and of a woman, Milena, both pregnant with demonic forces. The novel has gone through several editions and has been adapted for the stage in a highly acclaimed production by João Brites.*

Works by Hélia Correia

O Separar das Águas, *1981*
O Número dos Vivos, *1982*
Montedemo, *1983*
Villa Celeste, *1985*
A Pequena Morte/Esse Eterno Canto, *with Jaime Rocha, 1986*
Soma, *1987*
A Fenda Erótica, *1988*
A Casa Eterna, *1991*

THE DEVIL'S MOUNTAIN

For a long time, no one dared speak of the St. George's festival. Some, locked from within by a great shame, others treasuring voluptuously and avariciously the incommunicable memory of pleasure. Irene alone broke into fits of laughter, her back to the sea, stretching her arms in the direction of the mountain which could not be seen but could be imagined beyond the hills: greenish-black, shrouded in the sleep of a lamenting beast, of a shackled bear, with blood animated solely by longing, by its ancient instinct to pulsate.

In town, the tides vaporized: iodine and salt stinging the air. The days stretched out, lighting distances. And old men sat on the benches, with their enormous transparent ears, their lavender hands, expectantly awaiting the sun.

It was in these early days of the sultry season that the disappearance of Ercilia caused apprehension. She was a person often

---

From *Montedemo* (*The Devil's Mountain*), by Hélia Correia (Lisbon: Ulmeiro, 1983).

seen on the esplanades, knitting enormous yellow pieces, taking in the secrets of passers-by with the little eyes of a predatory bird. A bit behind her, engulfed in the shadow that always covered her like a gauze, her niece pressed her fingernails into her knees, half-blinded by the harsh sounds of summer. Her severe visage, earth-colored with bushy brows and tired mouth, remained expressionless throughout the afternoon, with only a nod to the aunt's friends who approached and remained until tea time.

But the balsam was at its peak, foreigners were beginning to arrive with light little hats and juvenile shouts, women arranged themselves with crochet and malice at the tables in the square—and dona Ercilia remained enclosed in her grave and musty first-floor apartment.

Guests and the cleaning woman had ready-made explanations for the mystery: rheumatism, laziness, swelling of ankles. And above all, a profound revulsion towards café conversation. It seems that she experienced crises of violent religious passion, though even going to mass became intolerable. The priest went in person to excuse her attendance: to confess her and to remind her, between sighs, that these days there are no rich parishes.

Thus tranquilized, disillusioned, the town turned its attention to Milena. They saw her, at dusk, walk along the coast with a light step, a flutter of skirts, lingering as if in an effort to repeat each step, to keep from being swallowed in the air.

And she crossed the streets with a daring breast like that of a wild mare. Her flashing eyes, fearfully beautiful, black and luminous like bewitching waters.

—She must be thirty-something—murmured the men in groups on the corners. Thirty-something, and it is only now that she is raising doubts . . .

—Thirty and a lot. And a lot! An unsalted little loaf—said the pharmacist—and look at what a woman from night to day! What you see there are a lot of vitamins.

They were summer months, abounding in winds, saturated with dust and aridity. All day long Milena paraded an unexpected and alarming beauty. In her tracks, the men's anxiety clashed with the women's envy. Irene had taken to following her, shuffling, persistent, with a blissful smile.

HÉLIA CORREIA

Through the Ferrão sisters Ercilia learned that her niece's innocent travels were alarming souls, to the point where a haze of sin could be felt hovering over the streets.

The old woman was shocked, since she had barely noticed Milena's absences, much less the belated splendor of that body. She lived absorbed in herself, in arduous prayer to atone for dreams in which men with naked shoulders threw her down on a mound of lottery tickets.

She began to follow her niece, to sniff her clothes, from which arose nauseating vapors. Intently, for hours, she worked with a knife to make a slit in the door of Milena's room.

Seven nights in a row, while the moon became full, she watched her lie on the cotton bedspread and fall asleep with her unbearable and tranquil smile. Until, bathed in gentle moonlight, Milena undressed and her rounded belly, tense and resplendant like mother-of-pearl, shocked the spying eyes of Ercilia. It was the belly of a pregnant woman.

The chaste woman became almost speechless. And to no one did she reveal the true cause of the humiliation to which she now condemned herself. The niece would pass by the cleaning woman, by old friends who visited, with only a slight glance to be interpreted as greeting. She ate little, went to the kitchen to chew mint, poultry parts. Her austere colorless outfits seemed light, vivid, molded to her breasts, twisting around her legs with a glitter, satin caresses.

When her belly began to swell arrogantly beneath her skirts and the town became astonished by the prodigy, Milena abandoned the house where she had grown up. Exactly two minutes before Ercilia decided to evict her, feeling, because of the pain that lashed her temples, that henceforward neither person nor force would oblige her to make decisions about or even acknowledge lamentable or hostile things. It was then that she became endowed with a selective deafness, so that her ears would decipher only happy words and any bad news or mere discomfort would come up against awkward incomprehension.

On that serene June afternoon, preparing herself in vain for tearful reactions and fictional scenes, the old woman crossed the corridor. It seemed to her that, in the dark, green lights sparked like the eyes of a feline. She was afraid and blessed herself, thinking that battles between God and the Devil were engaged in

THE DEVIL'S MOUNTAIN

such proximity to human beings that at times they were evident to the unprotected eye. She entered her niece's room and saw, in the coastal twilight, the unmade bed, the ransacked closet, the open drawers fallen on the floor.

—So, she's gone. So much the better—commented dona Ercilia. And she rested her left hand on her breast, to comfort an empty heart.

From one day to the next the town learned that Milena had taken up residence in the village idiot's shack. It was far to the south, in the shelter of the dunes and the reeds, made of crate slabs on mica. Irene intensified her begging for money and food from the vacationers, assaulted the tourists with catastrophic gestures, pulling her hair, having convulsions that entertained and disturbed them, doubling their reason for giving her charity. She went with old cans to the rear of hotels and waited for them to throw her scraps. And late at night she invaded orchards, stealing fruit and quieting the dogs through means that nobody was able to determine.

Milena never again approached the houses. Some boys said that they had seen her on deserted beaches where no one went other than for salty exaltations of flesh with French women seeking adventure.

They saw her on the dunes or, further away, breaking the surf. With agile golden legs, proud like columns supporting the earth. She skipped and smiled, stopping at times with her head bent over her breast. And there emanated from her, from her face, from her goat's flight, an ardor so strong that couples who chanced to observe her consumed themselves in never-experienced appetites. Which determined that the dunes, as had previously been the case with certain stones or nodes, would thenceforth be considered Aphrodite's blessings. Inducing in bodies more ardor than would egg yolks in honey or onion stew.

Aside from these sightings and Irene's excursions between shack and town, during those warm months, there were no contacts. Unnerved, sleepless, with dilated nostrils, restaurant and snack bar owners beat the pavements sniffing the traffic, the abundant cash.

New conquistadors, shielded only by their own light, the tourists spill through the streets. They imitate, laugh, photograph, spend. They rent rooms, buy aprons, making their way through their covetousness.

Bustling through that courtship, the townspeople hardly noticed those birds, gulls of a snowy and sad blue that came to die on the rocks. And only months later did they read bad omens in the voices that were heard on certain nights, enclosed in the density of fog, like the sound of someone who suffered pain or loved intensely on the beds of the sea.

At the end of September, Tenorio the pharmacist got the feeling that Irene was asking for help. She followed him, spied on him, hesitantly, as though limping under a weight. And on her homely ageless face gleamed the pallor of anxiety. Tenorio packed a bag and at dusk set off for the beach with a childish fear in his heart.

He walked unhurriedly until he lost sight of the last fisherwomen's huts. He was excited and remorseful because he had impiously forgotten Milena and her pregnancy during the dense summer months.

He sighted the shack where the sun wrapped itself in a gray and heatless circle. A frigid breeze came off the water, pricked with immaterial lights that absorbed color and luminosity. When he drew the curtain over the door, he recognized the warm and acrid air of animal beds. And even before he sighted Milena a profound peace, like a sudden release, deadened the vibration of his nerves. Only through the cracks in the wood did a lilac breeze occasionally blow. It was Irene's nervousness: she hovered, hidden in the night shivering, made inoffensive in those grandmother-fears.

—Wait—said Milena—I'll turn on a light.

She smiled then, immersed in an orangey and tremulous energy. At times, she appeared to be covered with resin, with a condensation of light amber. The flame of the candle in a can struck the walls with outsized forms. And all was round and throbbing like a risen dough, an aroused breast.

Tenorio found a seat on a box and heard the rustling of the hay on which Milena had reclined to speak to him. He was able to see then her macerated face and her indecipherable beauty. Still, she was only a woman alone animated by an independent life.

—I came to see you because of course—Tenorio explained—it will be necessary to prepare things. You will have to go to the hospital. . . .

SHIMMERING UMBRELLAS

He stopped, embarrassed, somnolent. There was no doubt that outside the shack the wind whirled and distended itself in divine rage, like a colt. But inside there was a sweetness, a memory of sea chests, of ship holds. Milena laughed and looked at him kindly:

—It's too bad you bothered. He'll be born here.

And from the sound of her voice, from the dilation of the nostrils, Tenorio knew that everything had been said. In any other circumstance of his life, he would have insisted, invoking reason. But the train of his own thoughts created connections that even he did not know. As if it were all very simple and memory made him lose time.

—That's fine. I'll come by every day.

He examined her with the circumspection of a doctor. He was whistling when, on taking leave, he took two vials from his bag. At the door, he stopped in the darkness.

—Have a fire and clean water always ready. Fire and a lot of clean water—he repeated.

Nothing had told him about the proximity of Irene but he was sure that he had only to turn fast to touch her.

Tenorio felt himself rejuvenate with those clandestine visits. His thin bachelor's life had flowed until then like lymph: without taste, vaguely repulsive. He had reached almost middle age through innumerable droughts, embellished from time to time with passions so internal that only the abnormal size of his arteries revealed them.

He was well read and had political convictions that had annoyed the dictatorship and now put him in conflict with all governments. Whatever they were, he would say, he was against them.

—There is no rain that does not wet nor power that does not oppress. It has been that way throughout history—he repeated. He took cold showers at five in the morning to rid himself of fears that assailed him. He feared the waiting and the solitude of death.

He thought of women as alien beings, viscous and quarrelling creatures who came into the pharmacy at all times with their hands in a gesture of adoration. He waited on them with severity, more knowledgeable than the doctors, experienced. He had never been in love and his orgasms were sensations, pure, absolute, without interference from the imagination. With friends, on the benches of the square, he let out impassioned sighs. Unnecessarily, since the others saw him as an extraordinary being, asexual, a brain implanted in a body not subject to the laws of organisms.

Age—that was hardly noticeable since he had never known how to look young—saturated him with knowledge. He had affective weaknesses that no-one had noticed because, coming from him, they would be so shocking, even so dubious, that the town preferred to disregard the discomfort. He gave the children menthol drops and fed old vagrant dogs.

He devoted himself to Milena in such a lively way that he had to exert himself to remove from his eyes a revealing gleam. He yearned for closing time at the drugstore and when they nabbed him for nighttime get-togethers, he stretched out the dinner hour. He would head toward the sand with his chest contracting from cold and tenderness.

Near the shack was Irene, her skirt snapping in the wind, glued against the night, mute and dark. Tenorio could not see her face but he felt, in the brusque ardor of the breeze, that she was waiting for him anxiously.

Milena received him smiling, with her enormous belly and hallucinating face, painful at seeing itself like the face of God. He brought her clothes, meals. And stood, rocked by vertigo, marvelling at the harmonies that exist in the pulsating of the blood, at the fantastic fragrance of the skin.

The first rains of autumn were falling when Tenorio received a message form Dulcinha Ferrão, making an appointment. In contrast to Isaura, who was delicate, Dulcinha was heavy and large-boned, a sergeant, they said, mocking her serious voice and her warrior's fuzz. Ironically, as a younger sister, she had never rid herself of the diminutive that was as inappropriate as a silk bow on her head. She lived with Isaura, who taught children and made a point of acquiring possessions, since she had already lost hope of finding a husband. Sterilized in that life, lonely and driven by religions in which they had tasted four heterodoxies, they cultivated naturism. And they helped dona Ercilia who, between crises of idiocy, continued to be interested in household medicine.

THE DEVIL'S MOUNTAIN

On the outskirts of the town, on a dark night, Tenorio saw Dulcinha approach him and thought with relief that they couldn't see each other's features. She spoke to him without hesitation:
—Take me to see Milena. I've thought a lot about her. Besides you, a woman is needed there.

He asked no questions since it seemed to him that the hours were passing quickly and the time reserved for interrogations was already past, swallowed up, annihilated. He thought only that he was no longer alone and that the unattractive body of Dulcinha filled innumerable vacuums.

Irene also felt relieved with that feminine presence. She began to make herself more visible and finally entered the shack with them.

The long walks along the beach, hiding their faces from the wind, soon became for Dulcinha and Tenorio joy and love. So much the more fervent since they themselves knew that they were evading the jaws of old age, laughing and imitating twenty-year-old coquetry.

In short, returning slowly, perhaps because they carried with them vestiges of a fascination with Milena, they immersed themselves in kisses and moans, disdaining the potential embarrassment of being observed.

When Isaura, breaking her timidity, told her sister that she detected something odd about her and that the neighbors were finding it strange to see her go out at sunset without fail, Dulcinha announced that she was getting married. And she looked at herself in the mirror, so self-absorbed that she didn't even say to whom.

It was around that time that the fires began in spite of the rain and put themselves out before the firemen had even a chance to intervene. They seemed to be ineffectual fires dripping from the roofs like liquid gold or solar feathers. They passed into the kitchens and melted buckets, bowls, everything that was made of plastic. Without discriminating, night after night, they upset lowland houses or the rich dwellings on the hillsides: forming cheerful leaping tails, or flowers of flame, or comets.

Seven nights these apparitions lasted, leaving only as a memory and as damage the amoeboid forms, like lava, like

HÉLIA CORREIA

coagulations of caramel—of melted plastic objects; thick colors, porous, repellent, fallen on the tables and on the floors, advancing tentacles, suspended in a transitory immobility. They had been roses and leaves, clothespins, funnels, boxes.

Even—and this was very frightening—figurines of saints, crucifixes, the ladies of Fatima with their fluorescence had been deformed like wax, taking on the gray color of bones.

Now, Tenorio having refused to give his explanations for such events, he who had always calmed his countrymen with his intransigent erudition; he himself wearing a smile and an impatience that revealed him naked as a child—his clandestine escapes, his meetings with Dulcinha, the purchases of both that included diapers and bibs, became the center of suspicion. The most irritated lamented that the return of the cold and the dormancy with which the town tried to compose itself after the excesses of the tourist months had allowed things to happen without benefit of vigilance and derision.

Never was a mystery so easy to clear up, since Dulcinha and Tenorio were as if in another dimension, breathing moon breezes, half blind to all that was not their love and Milena's delivery.

Thus were their steps followed by women, children, fishermen, one overcast nightfall when from the sea one gleaned only the hoarse pant of a sleeping male. The only sign in the darkness was the candle with which Irene guided the visitors from afar. But, sniffing out the crowd that followed them, the woman howled with such distress that the interlopers blessed themselves and stopped short, struggling to light cigarette lighters, matches, against the whirlwinds that surrounded them. They immediately recovered the strength to return to town with a shrug of the shoulders, prepared to reduce the story to household dimensions. Not even the Pope would make them confess that Irene had frightened them more than the storms.

Milena appeared not to be intimidated, and amused her friends at the expense of the terror and the courage between which the masses oscillate.

—Tomorrow—she said—some will come in the daytime. Others afterwards, and then they'll lose interest.

She was wrapped in a green wool coat that gave her belly the contours of a hill. And her large lignite eyes fixed on something vague, inattentive.

—Dulcinha's honor is what was destroyed—offered Tenorio—I know that those things aren't so important these days. But going off in the night with a man along the beach . . .

Dulcinha, who was heating up some carrot soup, felt herself blush like an adolescent.

—Now there's no remedy—she said.

—It's not a sickness—observed Milena—I would swear that you never felt so good. Why talk about a remedy? Love each other.

Irene, crouched near the fire, sensed that beneath the silence suddenly spread through the shack, there were entanglements, urgencies, joys. She had just begun to sing and to clap her hands when Milena became pale and announced that her son was about to be born.

Translated by Alice R. Clemente

THE TRANSLATORS

Susan Brown, who was trained in comparative literature, has done major work on the poetry of Fernando Pessoa. In her doctoral dissertation, she explored the influence of Walt Whitman on Pessoa's work. She has also published, in collaboration with Edwin Honig, two books of Pessoa translations: *The Keeper of Sheep* and *Poems of Fernando Pessoa*.

Alice Clemente, Professor of Spanish and Portuguese and of Comparative Literature at Smith College, has a long-standing interest in Portuguese women's fiction. She has authored individual essays on Sor Violante do Ceu, Agustina Bessa-Luís, Lídia Jorge, Eduarda Dionísio, Maria Ondina Braga, and Olga Gonçalves, and is now writing a book on the period covered by this anthology.

Charles Cutler, Associate Professor of Spanish and Portuguese and of Afro-American Studies at Smith College, works primarily on modern Brazilian literature and film. He has translated Thiago de Mello and Luis Rafael Sánchez and is at present studying the influence of popular culture on the work of Lima Barreto.

Francisco Fagundes, Professor of Spanish and Portuguese at the University of Massachusetts, has authored three books on Jorge de Sena: *A Poet's Way With Music: Humanism in Jorge de Sena's Poetry, Jorge de Sena: Art of Music* (with James Houlihan), and *In the Beginning There Was GENESIS: The Birth of a Writer*. He has also published over two dozen articles on topics ranging from Fernando Pessoa to Luso-American folklore.

Alexis Levitin, who has taught in Brazil and Portugal as well as at several colleges and universities in the United States, is at present on the faculty of the State University of New York at Plattsburgh. His translations of contemporary Brazilian and Portuguese poetry and short prose have appeared in well over one hundred literary magazines, including the *American Poetry Review, Latin American Literary Review,* and *Fiction.* He has translated three books of poetry by Portugal's Eugenio de Andrade: *Inhabited Heart, White on White,* and *Memory of Another River.* A fourth volume is forthcoming. His translation of Clarice Lispector's short stories entitled *Stations of the Body* has been published by New Directions. Earlier translations have appeared in numerous anthologies, including Macmillan's *Women Poets of the World,* New American Library's *Latin American Literature Today,* Prentice-Hall's *Women in Literature,* and the *Longman Anthology of World Writing by Women.*

Kim Marinus studied Portuguese at Smith College and later received a Master of Arts degree in comparative literature from the State University of New York at Binghamton. She was the library director at the Bryant Free Library in Cummington, Massachusetts, from 1977 to 1978, and is currently working at North Adams State College. She and her artisan-husband Charles live in a house that they built themselves in the beautiful hill country of western Massachusetts.

George Monteiro is Professor of English and Professor of Portuguese and Brazilian Studies at Brown University. His recent books are *The Correspondence of Henry James and Henry Adams, 1877-1914* (1992), *A Man Smiles at Death With Half a Face* (1991)—a translation of José Rodrigues Miguéis's *Um Homem Sori à Morte—Com Meia Cara, Robert Frost and the New England Renaissance* (criticism, 1988), *Self-Analysis and Thirty Other Poems by Fernando Pessoa* (translations, 1988), and *Double Weaver's Knot* (poetry, 1989).

TRANSLATORS

Naomi Parker holds an M.A. in Creative Writing and an M.A. in Portuguese and Brazilian Studies, both from Brown University. She is currently teaching Portuguese at Rhode Island College and working toward her Ph.D. in Portuguese at Brown. She is also translating Vergílio Ferreira's novel *Para Sempre* and preparing a manuscript of her poems.

Darlene Sadlier is Associate Professor of Spanish and Portuguese and Women's Studies, and Director of the Luso-Brazilian Program at Indiana University-Bloomington. She is the author of *The Question of How: Women Writers and New Portuguese Literature, Image and Theme in the Poetry of Cecília Meireles*, and *Cecília Meireles e João Alphonsus*. Her articles have appeared in *Novel, Studies in Short Fiction, Letras Femeninas,* and in literary reviews in Portugal and Brazil.

Nelson Vieira, Professor of Portuguese and Brazilian Literature and Director of the Center for Portuguese and Brazilian Studies at Brown University, specializes primarily in contemporary Brazilian literature. He has authored essays on Dalton Trevisan, Roberto Drumond, Clarice Lispector, Jorge Amado, Moacyr Scliar, Machado de Assis, and others. Among his published translations are Bernardo Santareno's *The Promise* and several Portuguese and Brazilian short stories. He is co-editor of the international literary journal *Brasil/Brazil*. His book *Brasil e Portugal, A Imagem Recíproca* was published in Portugal in 1991.

Renata Wasserman is Associate Professor of English and Comparative Literature at Wayne State University. She was born and raised in Brazil and educated in Brazil and the United States. Her specialty is nineteenth-century prose. She has written and published articles on George Eliot, Flannery O'Connor, and, more recently, on José de Alencar, Mário de Andrade, J. Fenimore Cooper, and René de Chateaubriand. She is currently working on a book about the expression of national consciousness in literatures of the New World, with emphasis on nineteenth-century fiction in the United States and Brazil.